POWER PLAYS

AN ALEXIS SHIPPERDOOM NOVEL

BOOK 1

JD BROYHILL

Copyright © 2023, 2025 JD BROYHILL
All rights reserved.

The characters and events portrayed in this book are fictitious. Any similarity to real persons, living or dead, is coincidental and not intended by the author.

No part of this book may be reproduced, or stored in a retrieval system, or transmitted in any form or by any means, electronic, mechanical, photocopying, recording, or otherwise, without express written permission of the author.

Without restricting the author's exclusive copyright rights, any use of this publication to "train" generative artificial intelligence (AI) technologies for text generation is explicitly forbidden.

ISBN-13: 9798992673241

Printed in the United States of America

Library of Congress Control Number:
2025904951

Dedication

To James, Jeremy, and Stephen—Never stop dreaming and believing.

To Rick—It never would have happened without you.

‘Sometimes it is best to be Queen…. the power is wonderful!’

~Alexis Snipperdoom

CONTENTS

The Beginning

"The weekly Witches meeting must be postponed. High Council Leader Grand Witch Alexis Snipperdoom has just given birth to her first child—it is a girl! We must visit at once and perform the Ritual of Newcome."

"Who will convey this important announcement to the entire council? We need to share this information right away. Our Clan has long awaited this moment. Yes, our first Grand Princess of Witches. This is a groundbreaking and historic development. Surely, others will now be inspired to follow our lead."

"Agreed!"

"We will immediately make the proclamation. We must then visit Grand Witch Alexis to meet our future leader, the Princess Witch. What is the child's name? What are we to call her?"

"Her name is Lilah, Grand Princess of Witches of the Lunar Council."

CHAPTER 1

Alexis sprawled on the bed like a Queen. Yes, she was royalty—Queen of Witches. It was something new for the council and realm of Alstromia. At the beginning of the new solar year, she was elected Queen of Witches to the Lunar Council. This new title became an essential step in making Alstromia more powerful.

Never had there been such a change in leadership. The control had been taken from a Warlock and given to a Witch! The regime change was Alexis's idea. She desperately desired a new kingdom rule. She wanted to make history, needed power, and felt Witchcraft was not enough. She truly was the most selfish of all Witches and was known throughout her council as one with a cold heart. Many loved her evil ways. Others despised her. Either way, Alexis did not care. She was fully aware of her reputation and planned to use it to her advantage.

The Queen of Witches had just given birth to her first child, a stunning baby girl. She was the new Princess and future leader of all Witches of Alstromia. Alexis and Armbruster, her husband, were overjoyed about the arrival of their heir. Armbruster, the head Chief of Warlocks, fell in love with Alexis the first time he met her at the Annual Meeting of Power. They married within a month of dating and announced the birth of their first child a year and a half later. They were a powerful team, and many feared their leadership, while others respected them.

Alexis rolled onto her side as Armbruster walked into her chamber to hand her Lilah, the little Princess sleeping in his arms.

"She is beautiful, isn't she?" asked Alexis, gloating. "Do you think she looks at all like me? You realize she will be Queen one day! She should and must look regal!"

"Oh, Alexis, she is just a child. Look at her. She is perfect in every way. She is such a blessing to the entire council and us. Why are you so worried? She will be a powerful Queen one day, just like her mother. The child's appearance does not matter. She will become a great leader and will be strong and beautiful. Give her a chance. Lilah will be our future leader, and you will teach her well." Armbruster frowned, staring at Alexis as she rolled her big, green eyes at him. She was obviously unhappy with his comments and never hid her displeasure.

"Armbruster, you are too soft. Some days, I simply cannot understand your whining and attitude. One day, she will be a leader of a new era. I know, without a doubt, Lilah will be superior. I can only hope she won't be as soft as you. You used to be such an authoritative and respected Warlock. Now, sadly, you are soft and only speak of peace and hope. I am hopeful she has the heart of steel that I possess. I find weakness a downfall, and I will not allow that!" Alexis cradled Lilah in her arms and smiled.

"Why do you talk like that, Alexis? You have changed, my dear. I cannot comprehend what you are doing. You used to be so sweet and kind. What has made you so stoic and cold?" Armbruster was less than pleased with Alexis and her attitude. He noticed many changes in her, none of them endearing. He feared her new position was going to her head, and she took everything too seriously. Armbruster felt Alexis needed to calm down, allowing the rest of the council to do their jobs and stop worrying about making so many drastic changes at once.

Alexis gently placed the child on the bed and stood up. She walked toward Armbruster and stood in front of him. Angry, she lifted her long finger and pointed it right in his face, almost touching his nose.

"I am not cold. This council wants to make us Witches something sweet and kind. We are not meant to be that way. We need to be feared and maintain control over others! This is why I am Queen. Sometimes, it is best to be Queen…the power is wonderful! This is why I am here. Anything else is just a waste of time. For generations, we have tried to blend into the real world. Enough! Let's make a stand and show our power."

She turned, walking back to the bed to pick up Lilah. Her anger softened as she gazed into her child's eyes. The infant was truly the most stunning baby. She had a full head of black curls and big, pouty pink lips.

Her unique eye color was a shade of lavender-gray. Lilah's adorable little, chubby cheeks made Alexis smile. Everything about the baby was regal and unique. Alexis knew she produced the most gorgeous heir and was highly pleased with herself.

"You are boring me, Armbruster. You are not the man I met and fell in love with...," Alexis announced with a frown. Though Armbruster's physique was quite intimidating at times, she was not impressed. Yes, he was tall and handsome. Some might even describe him as quite a catch. On occasion, some of the other Witches eyed him with pure lust. He stood tall, well over six feet, muscular and toned with broad shoulders. He had dark blue eyes, bushy yet well-groomed eyebrows, long and strong arms, a light brown complexion, and an incredible smile. He carried himself confidently, the one quality Alexis liked more than others.

Armbruster shook his head in disgust. He did not know what was happening to his wife and the love of his life.

"Darling, I feel you should rest. You are too exhausted to vent such energy. I shall leave you and Lilah alone. The council is on its way to perform the Ritual of Newcome. Please, be properly dressed for it. I will not tolerate any more nonsense from you today."

Having said what was on his mind, he turned and exited the chamber, heading down the corridor. His mind was ever wondering why Alexis changed. It worried him that perhaps childbirth was to blame for her change of character. *'Maybe she is ill?'* He grunted to himself as he walked on.

Enraged, Alexis placed Lilah on the bed and yelled for Carmin, Lilah's personal attendant. *'Who does Armbruster think he is, talking to me like that?'* True, she became Queen because of him, but by no means was he her equal. Just wait. Alexis would show Armbruster, the council, and the entire realm that she was in charge! Alexis was ready to unleash the new surprises she had plotted with Aerianna.

Carmin ran straight to the Queen's royal chamber. She knew better than to take her time. It would only result in trouble. She gently knocked on the door and entered the room. The Queen stood infuriated by the window. Alexis turned to her and pointed to the bed.

"Get Lilah ready. I do not want to be late. Have her dressed and bring her to the Hall immediately. Do you understand?" Alexis glared at Carmin.

"Yes, I understand, Your Majesty. I will do so immediately." She gently picked up the child and left the room. She walked down the hall to the next chamber, Lilah's room, and placed the Princess in her white crib.

The crib's bottom was padded with Pink Fluff, a soft and light material found growing on Trimbers along the Enchanted Wall. Trimbers resembled trees on Earth but were found exclusively on Alstromia, a planet a blink away from Earth, inhabited only by W3s—Witches, Wizzards, and Warlocks. The planet remained untouched by humans and was not visible to the human eye.

Carmin walked to the wall closet and opened the massive, white doors. Inside hung a variety of gorgeous gowns, handspun by the best and most-talented Witches. Alexis commissioned the best weavers to make the gowns when she learned she was having a child.

Carmin reached for a gown encased in a clear wrap. The long dress was light purple with tiny pink crystals and simply stunning. She opened a drawer and pulled out a pair of matching shoes. The sparkling tiara in the drawer elicited a smile from Carmin. She beamed with delight as she changed Lilah's clothes and placed the delicate crown on her head.

Trumpets blared in the background, announcing the arrival of other council members and visitors. Carmin knew she had to hurry to take the child to the Hall. She placed the baby in the silver Narry, an egg-shaped floating carriage. She walked along the corridor with the Narry and the resting child, humming and grinning the entire way to the auditorium.

Meanwhile, in Council Hall, there was a lot of chatter surrounding the arrival of the new Princess and the grand announcement the royal couple was about to make. Several Warlocks helped Witches find their chairs.

In the background, a large stage held two massive chairs and a silver mini-throne intended to hold the Narry, displaying the child to the Council. Three wide, glistening steps led up to the stage. Behind the stage, the scene was spectacular. A massive, open window showcased the picturesque and lush Valley of Grandu below the cliff. Trimbers lined the River of Miccay, which flowed softly with its usual dark gray water. Little huts of commoners lined the embankment. Further upstream, you could see the magnificent City of Miccay. It was where most council members resided.

The secure Palace of Snipperdoom sat high in the hills, surrounded by large Trimbers, only accessible by flying Torrins, a horse-like animal. At first glance, these majestic beings seem to radiate an iridescent glow from their predominantly gold bodies. Up close, their clear, crystal eyes resembled flawless diamonds.

Torrins, anxious by nature, flailed their shiny, sleek, black wings and manes when in flight, looking magical. Under the perfect conditions, as the moonlight struck their fur, a mesmerizing purple glow emanated from them. Torrins, wild and untamed, usually required immense training. However, their keeper and trainer, Collan, was an extremely gifted commoner, hand-selected by Alexis. He had a natural way with Torrins. Collan quickly gained their trust and could tame the beasts without much effort.

The Torrins' tails showcased giant pearls from the Sea of Miccay, found off the city to the east. These regal creatures were housed in an enormous stable adjacent to the Palace grounds.

Approaching the stable, you could see it was constructed from Trimbers, gray and black, with large, oval windows to accommodate the Torrin's heads. The tall, double doors granted entrance. They were built using Ozar, a metal strong enough to contain the feisty Torrins.

Once inside, you were greeted by vast rows of stalls. This building housed up to eighty Torrins. Alexis allowed the Torrins to deliver the visitors to her Palace, though their primary function was transportation for Alstromia's Security Command Team members.

"Attention, council members. Please find a seat and be silent. The Queen is about to enter the Hall. Please pick up the scrolls on your seat to acquaint yourself with the OOE (*Order of Events*)," announced Yarlen, the Second-in-Command of Warlocks.

He was an elderly Warlock with fluffy, gray hair pulled back into a long, braided ponytail. He wore the robe of Warlock Command in purple and blue. The grand robe was woven from the best Trimber material. He stood behind the King's seat and awaited the arrival of the commanding pair. He held the Ceptre of Argin, with its dark blue center, swirling in a circular motion, giving off a white, intense light. The Ceptre signifies power, and others greatly respect it.

Armbruster gifted Yarlen the Ceptre with its magical *'seeing sphere'* as part of his change of power ceremony. Owning this magical Ceptre, identified Yarlen as Head Seeier of Alstromia. He is the only one to see changes in the sphere. The Ceptre is believed to allow Yarlen to view the future or see both good and bad special events.

Quiet chatter continued until Armbruster walked through the door holding Queen Alexis's. He carefully guided her toward the throne and assisted her as she sat. She gave him a crooked smile and stared straight ahead at the rest of the council. Armbruster took a seat beside Alexis and folded his hands. He tucked his feet beneath his Warlock Command robe. Everyone remained silent. Yarlen quietly stepped away and sat in the front row, facing the Queen and her Warlock husband.

Within seconds, the door swung open again. The Narry was the first thing everyone saw, followed by Carmin. The eager crowd turned their heads to watch the arrival of the baby. Carmin walked into the room wearing her favorite lavender robe. Her long, black hair was pulled back into a massive bun. She smiled as she guided the Narry toward the stage. Once there, she snapped the Narry into the silver throne before Alexis and Armbruster. She stood behind the couple, remaining close but out of sight.

"Witches, Warlocks, Wizzards, council members, and visitors...it is my great pleasure to announce the arrival of my beautiful daughter and your future Queen, Grand Princess Lilah of the Lunar Council. Please, be so kind as to remain quiet as we induct her into our council and great Alstromia," Armbruster proclaimed.

He lifted the child out of the Narry and proudly displayed her for all to see. Ahhhhhhs and oooohs were heard throughout the Hall. Everyone was in awe of the child's undeniable beauty. The baby, now fully awake, looked attentively around the room and seemed to smile. Her eyes sparkled, and she appeared to hypnotize most.

Armbruster walked to the table by the window, holding Lilah tightly against his body. Alexis stood beside him, resting a hand on the child's arm. The head of the Council performed the Ritual of Newcome to welcome the child and officially give her the title of Grand Princess Lilah of the Lunar Council.

Once the short process was complete, Alexis kissed the child's forehead and asked Carmin to take her to Visitation Hall, where the celebration would continue shortly.

"I want to thank you all for your attendance. It is my pleasure to have you witness this new and exciting event—the introduction of your new Princess. Thank you all for your kind wishes. We thank you, as well, for the lovely presents you have bestowed upon us."

Alexis sat down on her throne and changed her demeanor. "Now, I must address a few necessary items. Surely, most of you are aware of the new Council and Order we have established. Some of you are visibly displeased with the changes. Let me be clear—if you do not like it, too bad! This is how it will be from now on. If you have issues with this leadership and council, feel free to move to Iriss. Perhaps you will like it better there? I am sure my sister, Zandorah, Head Witch of Solara Council, will happily welcome you to her Clan. I am not interested in having anyone on Alstromia who is unwilling to comply with the new rules and regulations. This leadership is looking to make history. If you do not want to be part of it, leave. I know this sounds harsh, but it is reality."

She stood up, walked down the three steps, and approached the seated council members in the front row. She stopped in front of Aerianna, her best friend, and smiled. "I request you to become my Second-in-Command. I want nothing more than to have you sit next to Armbruster and me as we plan the rest of the new changes. Please accept the new position," she stood impatiently, awaiting her response.

Aerianna smiled and rose quickly from her seat. She bowed to Alexis and raised her palm to receive the purple Gem of Elight. This gem was only given to those closest to Alexis, and receiving it was a huge honor. It would be worn in a special headpiece to signify membership in the Elite Council. Alexis placed the glittery gem into Aerianna's palm and cupped Aerianna's fingers around it. "So be it," she declared.

Alexis beamed with happiness as she turned to return to the throne. Finally seated, Alexis announced, "Please welcome Aerianna—Fanna of Alstromia…my Second-in-Command. She will be assigned elite security. I will expect you to treat her with the respect she deserves," Alexis watched as other council members and visitors congratulated Aerianna, some with apparent jealousy.

Rumors circulated on Alstromia, Draekidell, Earth, Iriss, and Xeagadale, implying Alexis planned to elect Aerianna. Still, no one knew for sure, mainly because most assumed Armbruster, her husband, would become the Queen's Second-in-Command.

However, Alexis felt Armbruster held too many other responsibilities as Head of Warlocks. She did not want to worry about his lack of attention to her needs and plans. She intended to make Aerianna her Second-in-Command because she realized Aerianna would do whatever she asked and wanted. Alexis spent hours contemplating how she would change the council and assign them new jobs in this historic and revolutionary leadership.

Armbruster continually whined about Alexis' vision and ideas. He reaffirmed her belief that keeping him out of her plans was best. It was a much easier plan this way.

Aerianna remained in the chair and held the precious gem. With a wicked grin on her face, she nodded at Alexis, feeling elated, knowing they would make a powerful pair. She shared a long history with the Queen. They grew up together and had always been a powerful combination. Aerianna knew in time that Alexis would officially make her part of the Council. She felt honored, dreaming of this moment and replaying the scenes in her mind over and over.

At night, she contemplated how she could help guide Alexis in her decision-making. It was an exciting time filled with endless possibilities. Aerianna knew she was not just a friend to Alexis but also someone who would help Alexis realize her goals and vision for the future of Alstromia. She was more than willing to sacrifice for her beloved friend, Alexis.

"Everyone, please be seated for one more moment. I have a final announcement to make. I want to thank you all for your attendance. I invite you to join us for a welcome banquet for Princess Lilah in Visitation Hall. We will also hold the Change of Title for Aerianna there at the same time," Armbruster announced.

"Yes, please, leave," Alexis chimed in, always insistent on having the last word. She looked at Armbruster with disgust. *'Why does he always have to speak?'* He greatly irritated her at times, and this was one of them. She turned her head away, frustrated with Armbruster.

The room fell silent as the Council and visitors left to proceed to the reception and the Change of Title ceremony.

Alexis stood up and strolled toward the window, surveying the scenery below. She felt elated, knowing she was in control. Now, she was convinced more than ever she'd made the right choice in selecting Aerianna for the position.

Armbruster tapped her arm and informed her it was time to join the others. She harshly pushed his arm away. "Go. Go ahead. I will stay here for a while, as I have a headache. I need some time to myself," she rolled her eyes, irritated. She ignored him, staring at the valley below.

Armbruster shrugged his shoulders, tired of Alexis and her foul mood. He exited the room to meet with his Warlock Command Team for a quick conference before attending the royal festivities. Armbruster refused to continue to coddle Alexis.

CHAPTER 2

Alexis sat on a tall, padded stool by the window, looking out. Feeling hopeful, she daydreamed of her future and the powerful, new kingdom. As she surveyed the valley, she wondered if all her plans would unfold smoothly.

She realized how much she disliked the view as she took in the scenery. The moment she arrived on Alstromia, she felt the region was much too cheery and bright. She simply did not care for it. The whole atmosphere needed a drastic makeover! She had every intention of changing the environment, as it fell short of her standards. She planned to make it the gloomy, dreadful place she had envisioned.

Alexis reluctantly agreed to erect her Palace at the highest point, Grandu Peak, overlooking the valley. She adamantly disliked the bright light and glorious scenery and was not impressed. She missed the dark valley on Earth, where she previously resided, loving the dark, musky castle in New England, America. As she thought about Earth's details, she realized one of the things she yearned for the most was the rumble and shaking of the mighty thunder, especially the bright flashes of lightning. She sighed as she reminisced about fighting with humans and playing wicked tricks on them. There was so much she missed.

Looking at the current scenery, she felt discontented. Somehow, Alexis had convinced herself she could start a new life on Alstromia and make it a better place for all Witches, Wizzards, and Warlocks, without human interference. She did not miss being harassed by humans or being hunted down like a wild animal. Humans were worthless creatures. She was glad she no longer needed to deal with them.

The night she fled Earth, she vowed never to return. So many had betrayed her. Alexis felt Earth was no longer a safe place to reside. Her quick departure was the best decision at the time. Armbruster, however, continued to express his dislike for their abrupt departure from the planet. He preferred to remain in contact with their friends and planned to visit them back on Earth.

Alexis adamantly disagreed with Armbruster. Somewhere or somehow, in her heart, she knew those humans would eventually turn on them as well. Humans could never be trusted. Sadly, she had learned this unfortunate lesson too many times before.

Armbruster believed in humans and admired their character. He thought they were trustworthy. Alexis felt Armbruster was very naïve. She despised his weakness and thought his trust in humans was misplaced.

Life on Alstromia was far better. It contained zero humans. She decided how it was run and who or what could visit or remain on the planet. Alexis believed she had gained complete control for the first time in her life. Now, all she had to do was get Armbruster to see it her way or dispose of him as well. She preferred not to get rid of him, as part of her still cared for him very much. Alexis felt torn between what she wanted and what had to be accomplished. It was never easy being the Queen of Witches.

Her gaze caught Torrins flying up to the Landing Deck, pulling the carriages, delivering Witches, Wizzards, and Warlocks to this monumental occasion. She spotted a few familiar faces. Aerianna stood below on the deck, welcoming VIPs to the event, mostly from other councils.

Aerianna was in her full glory. She looked stunning in her dark purple cloak. Her long, curly, blonde hair, which always seemed somewhat unruly, was draped down her back. However, the look seemed to work for her. She was a rather tall woman with long legs. Her face was breathtaking. She had full, bright-pink lips. Aerianna's eyes were a deep chestnut color. However, her most stunning feature was her amazing, long, and fluttery eyelashes. Aerianna was also very blessed with a tiny waist and a voluptuous body. Alexis had always been extremely jealous of Aerianna's gorgeous figure and features. However, she would never admit it to anyone.

The twin moons glistened in the darkening evening sky off in the distance, giving off an eerie glow while casting a soft light on the valley. The wind was soft and warm. It was a wonderful evening, which would be filled with fun, excitement, and most of all, unexpected events!

Not far away, Armbruster discussed the planned changes with his Command Team. He insisted on increased security, as some of the other councils would surely want to sabotage the new establishment about to take place on Alstromia. Armbruster was also highly concerned about Lilah and Alexis's safety.

He instructed the Guard of Command to be on high alert and ordered the team to circle the Palace on their Torrins, securing the perimeter. Armbruster did not want any interruptions while they celebrated and held the festivities. It was his responsibility to keep his wife and child safe. He worried more than most and never seemed to be able to relax.

Ever since leaving Earth, he felt a bit more relaxed, but still believed other councils (and Clans) wanted to sabotage all they were trying to establish on Alstromia. In his heart, he knew things would be great on Alstromia in time. For now, challenges lie ahead.

However, he still profoundly missed Earth and his human friendships. He wished Alexis would understand his need for human interaction and relationships. She scolded him about the humans and repeatedly demanded that he cease all communication with them at every opportunity. It irritated him.

Often, he thought about returning to Earth. However, now he had a child. He also still loved Alexis, though she had changed, not for the better. He sighed and looked into the distance, thinking about his time on Earth.

Alexis stepped away from the window and walked to her chamber. She changed robes, opting for her Grand Ceremony gown. It flowed to the ground with a purple, pearlescent glow. She picked up her silver, crystal-encrusted brush and ran it through her lustrous, black, hip-length hair, admiring herself. She was ecstatic that the visitors were about to witness part one of her new plan of change. It made her tingle with delight. Alexis realized Armbruster would disapprove, but she did not care. *'Too bad.'* Her eyes twinkled, and she felt a rush come over her. She was ready to make the changes of a lifetime.

Eager to begin the epic evening, she opened the closet and withdrew her tall Star Ceptre. The handle of the Ceptre had a lizard-like texture. Affixed to the top was a blood-red square-encrusted gem surrounded by tiny, glistening stars. When Alexis cast a spell or transported herself, she slammed down the Ceptre, causing the silver, sparkling stars to produce an opaque fog.

She raised the Ceptre to the ceiling and shouted, "In the name of Sonia, give me the power!" Instantaneously, she felt a small jolt vibrate through her from head to toe. She giggled and nodded gleefully as she walked toward the door. Briefly, she stopped, admiring herself. She gazed at the reflection in the floor-length mirror with self-adoration.

Alexis liked what she saw—beauty and power. *'What a great combination,'* she thought, realizing she was about to make history. She was not shy about expressing her vanity or denying how proud she was of her accomplishments. Alexis considered herself a visionary, believing she was set to become the greatest Witch ever! She left the room feeling confident, ready to start anew. She slammed the chamber door and rushed down the corridor, her cloak dragging behind her, making swishing sounds.

Armbruster sat at the head table in Visitation Hall. He gazed to the right side of the table and observed Yarlen speaking with Garlow, his son. Armbruster noticed Aerianna looking smug off to the left with her new Gem of Elight in her Elite Council Head Circlet. He did not like Aerianna, as he knew she was obsessed with power. She was always looking to make changes he felt were radical.

When Alexis unfolded her plans to bring Aerianna into the Elite Council, he became pretty annoyed. He was quite vocal, letting her know it was a colossal mistake, realizing his opinion was irrelevant to her. Alexis would not listen. She made up her mind, determined not to change it. She was simply informing him of her decision, not asking for his approval.

Alexis never asked. She did what she desired. At one point, it was something he admired about her, but now, it was the one thing he truly disliked. Having Aerianna as her Second-in-Command would only signal future problems. He disliked it immensely.

Aerianna knew what Alexis planned for the celebration, but was also keenly aware that Armbruster would become furious.

Regardless, she planned to support Alexis and her vision for change. Aerianna tapped her long fingernails on the side of the table as she awaited the Queen's arrival. As she scanned the room, she marveled at the sizeable crowd that had gathered. "What an impressive turnout," she mused. Aerianna felt pleased for Alexis and Lilah, but Armbruster was a different matter entirely.

Aerianna did not get along well with Armbruster and long ago realized it was better to stay out of his way. She kept her relationship close to Alexis and ensured she remained civil to Armbruster, only to appease the Queen. Aerianna knew that having Armbruster as an enemy could be disastrous. He still had many influential connections, and it was best not to mess with him. Aerianna was not stupid, after all. The Hall filled with laughter and talk.

The crowd seemed happy, boisterous, and unaware of what would shortly happen. Numerous local council members mingled with councils from other planets, including Earth. Many were busy looking for assigned seating around the big tables strategically placed throughout the room.

Wizzards, Warlocks, and Witches were separated and seated in order of command, by district or Clan. Other visitors sat in the back of the large room. Their view was not the best, but they could still see the event.

Security guards were in every corner of the room. They held Mesmer Ceptres, prepared to protect the Palace if necessary. They wore black, mid-length robes, with their trousers tucked into boots. Looking out the windows, one could see the Security Guard of Command patrolling on their flying Torrins, vigilantly circling the Palace. Security was at its highest level for this event, as ordered by Armbruster.

Alexis entered the reception area. Everyone immediately stopped talking and quickly took their seats. She strutted confidently toward her seat, stopping next to Armbruster. Alexis nodded at her Second-in-Command, and Aerianna reciprocated. Armbruster touched her hand gently, admiring his wife, only to have it swiped away.

"Not now," Alexis hissed with a frown and total impatience. *'Just you wait,'* she thought.

Carmin finally arrived with Lilah, who was sleeping in the Narry. No one spoke, watching quietly. Carmin placed the Narry behind Alexis and was dismissed. She approached a stool and sat, keeping an eye on Lilah. Armbruster stood up, clapping his hands.

"Witches, Warlocks, and Wizzards…may I please have your attention? I want to thank you again for your attendance. We will start our celebration with food and drinks, followed by the official Change of Title for Aerianna. Please have fun and enjoy this monumental event. This truly is an evening of celebration!" He sat down quickly, not wanting to extend it longer than necessary.

Suddenly, somewhere deep in his mind, he tried to dismiss the feeling as if something horrible was about to happen. Armbruster wanted this evening to be perfect. Something was wrong. He felt it deep in his gut. Instantly, Armbruster began to shake and feel nauseous, his right eye twitching uncontrollably. Concerned, he rubbed it briefly. Beads of sweat pooled over his bushy eyebrows. His face felt flushed as he heard his heart beating in his ear, thumping.

Everyone applauded his announcement. The large doors swung open, and the wait staff entered, pushing large carts overflowing with plates of food and drinks. Delicious smells permeated the room. The staff walked around, filling up tables to feed the hungry crowd. Other staff members filled the oversized glasses on the tables with famous potions, brews, and other concoctions, courtesy of Henrii Snubberly and the BrewHaus. Everyone in attendance seemed to be having a great time. It was a lively event.

Alexis surveyed the room, scooted close to Armbruster, cupping her hands over his ear, and whispered, "Enjoy this, my love. It is what we have waited for." She moved back to her seat and smugly winked at Aerianna.

She ran her right hand through her hair, pushing stray strands behind her ear. At times, she wished her hair were shorter. It was so annoying to have it fall over her eyes, blocking her view. *'Maybe I should cut it all off? No, probably not.'* She was just irritated. *'No need to do anything radical with my looks, for now,'* she thought.

Armbruster observed Alexis, perplexed. *'What did she mean by that comment? Is she sincere, or is it a mixed message?'* The bad feeling in his stomach grew. He muttered, "Excuse me, dear, I will be right back," he proceeded to stand up and walk toward his security team.

"I have an odd feeling in my stomach. Please have everyone on the lookout. I do not know what we are looking for, but something feels off. I do not want anything to ruin this evening. Have I made myself clear?" The head of the Security Council nodded, signifying he understood the responsibility. He swiftly walked off to talk with the rest of his team, barking out orders.

Armbruster turned and headed for the tall double doors in the back of the room. He also wished to check on the outside security team. However, as he attempted to open one of the doors, he discovered it was locked! Stunned, he spun around to see Alexis standing up.

Instantly, his heart skipped a beat, making him feel dizzy. He knew something horrific was about to happen. He stood in shock and disbelief, waiting to find out why she was standing, looking ever so self-righteous. He knew she was about to do something dreadful.

"Everyone, may I please have your attention? Armbruster, sit!" Alexis ordered. She motioned for him to sit, pointing to a chair with her long, bony finger. "I would like to inform everyone that I have ordered all doors locked. The windows are sealed, and no one leaves until I am done talking."

Instantly, everyone panicked, looking around nervously. Most did remain quiet, generally because they were scared and unsure of what was happening or what was about to happen.

"Aerianna, please come sit by me." She gestured to her friend and confidant. "I have decided to share my secret plan with all of you. Those of you here may or may not be part of it. However, you will not leave the Hall until you fully understand what I am about to do. You may decide where you want to be and if you wish to be part of this new plan."

Armbruster plopped down in the chair nearest to him, feeling weak, confused, and upset. He shook violently, pissed off. His gut feeling had been correct. Somewhere in his mind, he knew something was wrong. He hated the fact that he was right. He listened to Alexis, watching a woman he no longer knew. Armbruster was greatly disappointed. Alexis was out of control. He glared at Aerianna in disgust, knowing she had been up to no good, plotting this moment with Alexis.

Not long ago, Aerianna accepted Alexis's invitation to move into the palace to be near her side. Armbruster tried to convince himself that Aerianna was there simply to help Alexis during the difficult pregnancy. Now, he knew there was more to that story. He felt ill. Bile filled his mouth, and it made him feel horrible. He grabbed a glass filled with Porting Wine off a nearby table and guzzled it. He felt woozy. *'What is happening?'* The security team stood by and did nothing. He knew right then and there that she had arranged something with them. They were under her control, and he lost his power!

"As many of you know, I am sickened over the bright and sweet environment of Alstromia. We moved to Alstromia to start fresh. I do not want our new home to be so damn fluffy and happy. The current conditions do not reflect the true environment I had envisioned for our glorious Alstromia. We are Witches, Wizzards, and Warlocks, for goodness' sake! We are powerful and should be feared. We should not be subjected to this unsatisfactory and sunny atmosphere. With that said, I will cast a spell to change the planet to reflect a more appropriate environment immediately."

She raised her Star Ceptre and exclaimed, "Let the light reflect the mood. For now, I see what is good."

Suddenly, everything outside became black. Lightning flashed, adding an eerie glow to the dark night sky as loud, pounding rain poured out of dark clouds. Alexis squealed with delight.

Aerianna smiled and clapped with joy, much like a small child. Others looked stunned, only mumbling under their breath. Armbruster lowered his head and tried to keep himself from crying. He rubbed his pounding temples. He could not believe what was happening. Armbruster shook his head in disbelief and closed his eyes. Everything swirled around him.

"Finally, a proper atmosphere for our new adventure. I ask for your patience while the surroundings change. As I mentioned, if you are dissatisfied with the transformation, please consider relocating to Iriss, Earth, or perhaps even Draekidell or Xeagadale. As I understand, the Blud-Trackers will allow W3s to join them on their planets. Perhaps those of you who are weak may prefer to live under their leadership. If so, please step forward so we may transport you to Iriss as soon as possible. I do not want anyone weak in my Clan or council. So, rest assured, you may leave."

Armbruster stood up, waving at his wife. "Alexis, I beg you to reconsider. May we please talk privately?"

"I will speak with you later, Armbruster. You are not well. You are dismissed. Yarlen, take Armbruster to his chamber," she ordered. The large double doors unlocked, and Yarlen stood up, approaching Armbruster to guide him to his private chamber. As they exited, the doors closed with a bang and relocked.

"Anyone else feel like departing?" Alexis inquired. There was silence.

A short and stout Witch in the back raised her hand. "Grand Queen Alexis, I would like to be excused. I want to take my family to Iriss."

"So be it. Take your leave and never return. You will be destroyed if I see you in my Clan or near this planet again," hissed Alexis.

"Yes, very clearly. Thank you." The young Witch approached the doors. They popped open, allowing her to leave swiftly. The doors closed again, but this time remained unlocked.

"I invite all weaklings to leave immediately. This new kingdom is only for the strong and visionaries. You should not stay if you do not want any part of it."

Several Witches and Warlocks dashed to the door and hurriedly departed the Hall. After a few moments, no one else left, remaining seated quietly. Alexis stood up.

"Good, I see my loyal followers have stayed. Let me say thank you. You will not regret this decision. Let the new changes begin now." The light dimmed in the room. Next to the head table, the massive fireplace ignited with bright, purple, and green flames on the right side of the wall.

"Now, let's have some fun!" shrieked Alexis. She turned to Carmin and asked her to take Lilah to her room. "Please, watch over her and take a security officer with you."

"Yes, I will do so now," stated Carmin. She unsnapped the Narry and guided it out of the room toward Lilah's nursery. Once there, she instructed Pauto, a security officer, to stay and keep guard. He smiled and reassured her that all would be okay.

Alexis reassured Aerianna she would hold the Change of Title Ceremony privately later in her chamber. Aerianna honestly did not care when it would happen. She was thrilled that Alexis had finally made the public announcement about her intended changes for the Planet. Besides, she had what she wanted…the coveted title of Second-in-Command. That was all that truly mattered to her.

On the other end of town, near the river of Miccay, the three Warlocks met in secrecy. They huddled around a small, oval table in a dimly lit room. The commoner's cottage was the perfect, inconspicuous place to discuss their strategy.

"The plan is perfect! You morons better know your part. My future depends on it," bellowed the tall and muscular figure. He sat across the table, staring at the other two, squinting his eyes.

"Sir, it is brilliant. We know exactly what we have to do," replied Bartin, squirming in his seat.

"If you mess this up, you will be sorry. I cannot, and will not, allow you two to destroy all we have worked for…you better be prepared!" He slammed his fists down on the table, causing it to shake. Bartin apprehensively looked at his acquaintance, hoping he would say something. However, he remained silent, scared of any repercussions. He knew it was best not to say a word.

"If all goes well, I shall regain my power, and she will pay…"

In the chamber, Carmin dressed Lilah in her sleeping gown, placing the baby in the fluffy crib. She gently covered the sleepy child. Carmin proceeded to walk to her bed on the other side of the large room. She plopped down on the thick blanket and closed her eyes. It wasn't easy to comprehend what had just happened. She admired Alexis but now feared her. She wished Armbruster had done something to stop her, but realized he no longer had any form of control. Armbruster was weak, and Alexis won.

The noise of the rain pelting the window lulled Carmin to sleep. She heard echoes of thunder in the distance, reminding her of nights on Earth. She smiled as she drifted off into a deep sleep. She never heard the baby's soft cry as a tall, dark figure lifted Lilah from her crib.

CHAPTER 3

"Help! Help! OH NO...the Princess has been kidnapped!!" screamed Carmin. Frantically, she ran up and down the hallway looking for Pauto, or any other security member, almost tripping over her feet. As she turned the corner of the corridor, she bumped into Armbruster, causing him to hit the wall.

"What are you saying?" he screamed, violently clutching Carmin's arm. "Where is my child?" his eyes flashing in anger.

"Sir, last night, I placed the Princess in her crib. I woke up this morning to feed her, and she was gone. I rushed to the Queen's Chamber, thinking she might have the Princess, but she did not. Sir, Lilah is gone. I believe she was kidnapped!" Carmin fell to the ground, shaking and crying, her head buried in her hands, tears running down her cheeks.

Armbruster shook his head as he looked down at Carmin. *'Stupid and worthless woman! Why did she not protect my daughter?'* Fuming, he turned and sprinted down the hall. Just as he was about to turn another corner, he encountered a security commoner with a Mesmer Ceptre in his right hand. It appeared the security commoner was already aware of the missing child and had initiated a massive security sweep, scouring the Palace looking for the missing baby. Security was on its highest alert.

Still, Armbruster did not like the fact that the baby was still missing. Most likely, this meant she was not in the Palace—Lilah had been kidnapped. He became enraged. Quickly and forcefully, he pushed aside the security commoner and turned to find Alexis. She was undoubtedly in her chamber.

He never made it to her room as he spotted her approaching with pure anger on her face.

Alexis ran toward Armbruster and grabbed him by the arm. "What have you done?" she screamed at him. "My child is missing because you are weak. Find my daughter or pay the price." She released his arm and took a swing at him. He stopped her hand an inch before his face.

"Stop it, Alexis. You are out of control! I understand you're scared, but enough! Gain control of your emotions. Others are watching us," his eyes wide open, his bottom lip sticking out.

Frustrated and disgusted with Armbruster, she spun around and fled the area to seek out Aerianna. Armbruster was deathly afraid. He had no idea who had taken his child. *'The audacity,'* he thought. He wondered if it was someone close to him. Was it payback for Alexis and her new plan for the Clan? He felt ill all over again. If this were retaliation because of Alexis' grand new plan, she would pay, and he would personally see to it. Her irresponsible actions could have prompted the kidnapping.

Aerianna shook her head in disbelief as Alexis informed her about Lilah's disappearance. She was stunned and could not believe what she had heard. Somehow, Alexis seemed uncomfortably calm, considering her child was missing. It made Aerianna wonder how she was able to remain so cool.

"What will you do, Alexis? Who do you think took her? Why did they take her?"

"I cannot even try to guess. I will tell you one thing for sure: whoever took her will be sorry, and they better hope she is returned unharmed, or they will surely perish!" Aerianna watched as Alexis began pacing back and forth. She became more agitated as time progressed. Her demeanor changed rapidly.

Armbruster sat in a circle with four other Warlocks in another chamber, planning their next move. Orin, his trusted friend, explained that he had heard someone walking and making noise outside earlier in the morning and had ordered security to investigate.

Unfortunately, nothing unusual was found. Suddenly, the door blew open, and a breathless security member entered, struggling to speak. "Calm down, my friend. Take a moment," Armbruster advised.

"Sir, two of the Torrins and a carriage are missing. It is the Queen's carriage. It is gone! What are your orders, Sir?" he stood at attention, waiting to hear Armbruster's response.

"Please return to the security team and instruct them to take Torrins to conduct a security sweep. They must locate the missing carriage. I want it found immediately."

The security commoner bowed his head in acknowledgment and left swiftly. He was given a mission and would not fail. He dashed down the steep staircase to locate other security members and provide them with the new orders. Within minutes, seventeen young commoners mounted Torrins and flew off into the morning to find the missing carriage and Princess.

Meanwhile, Alexis succumbed to her misery, lounging in a chair by the window, crying. She rubbed her eyes. It had been a long time since she felt this out of control, and she greatly disliked it. Alexis grieved the disappearance of her daughter. *'Why did this happen?'* She seethed. *'It better have nothing to do with Armbruster,'* she thought. However, her gut feeling told her it had everything to do with him. Perhaps it was related to his growing incompetence as a leader. Armbruster was becoming a liability, and she knew she could no longer rely on him. Alexis would take things into her own hands. She would enlist Aerianna's help. She was more than capable.

Alexis realized the front of her gown was soaked with tears. She rose from the chair and walked toward her closet to change out of her wet attire. Searching through her wardrobe, she chose one of her favorites: a dark gray, flowing robe with purple crystals embedded in the sleeves and neck. She loved the feel of the material. It soothed her when she was upset. Once she wore the gown, she returned to her enormous, plush chair. She placed her head in her hands and sat quietly. Suddenly, Armbruster burst through the door with two guards behind him.

"I have news! We found one of the drivers of your carriage. Someone knocked him over the head, and he was unconscious. Now that he was awake, he informed the team that he had seen the face of the thief and claimed it was a woman. She wore a purple robe with silver Darbeds. You know, the only ones wearing Darbeds are the Witches from Earth!"

Immediately, Alexis stood up and walked toward Armbruster. "What are you saying, Armbruster? Do you believe it was my mother? Was it Lorthana? Answer me," she screamed hysterically.

She pointed her finger, almost touching his face, and continued her tirade, "If it is Lorthana, I will tell you this…she will perish by my hand. Mark my words." Clenching her fists, she pounded the air, grinding her teeth. Her eyes flashed like lightning from anger as she stared at Armbruster with a vicious scowl.

Alexis stormed off to the Royal Meeting Chamber, two security guards on her heels. Her black hair flowed behind her like a long, black veil. She was furious. *'How dare that woman?'* she thought. *'Why would Lorthana do this? Did she really think she would get away with kidnapping my child?'* Alexis would ensure the traitor paid with their life.

Opening the large, double doors to the royal Meeting Chamber, Alexis frowned. "Locate Aerianna and bring her here immediately!" she shrieked at Pershiah, her assistant. Pershiah appeared dumbfounded for a moment, staring at the Queen.

"Lazy girl, did you not hear me? Get off your big behind and go get her now." Scared to death, Pershiah ran from the chamber to find Aerianna. Alexis watched her quick departure, smiling and feeling amused.

At the same time, Armbruster appeared in the royal Meeting Chamber with his guards. He tightly held the *Book of Varathune* in his shaking hands. He looked deep in thought as he mindlessly tapped his middle finger on the book, glaring at Alexis.

"Alexis, we must read the Detector and possibly enact the *Chant of Reztec.* We must ensure the safety of the Clan and the kingdom. Please! I know you are upset. However, we need to protect everyone. If Lorthana took Lilah, then she will be okay. Lorthana will not harm our child. Plus, we do not even know for sure if she is the one responsible."

"You must think I am an idiot. Of course, it was Lorthana! My mother told me she would make me pay for betraying our family and leaving when we departed Earth. I believe this is her way of sending me a clear message." Alexis stood up from her chair and walked toward Armbruster. "Why do you insist on being so protective of her? Hmmm? What is it you know about this?" She squinted her eyes, observing him as she shook her head in disgust. He squirmed uncomfortably in his stance, still tapping the book.

"Exactly what are you accusing me of, Alexis?" he growled back, with his head cocked off to one side. He knew what she was implying, and it angered him. *'Why does she think I am shielding anyone? Why does she doubt my loyalty? I have not given her any reason to feel this way.'*

"Oh, let's not play games, Armbruster. You know what I am saying to you." She rolled her shoulders and continued keeping her eyes on him. She felt betrayed, standing before him with her hands on her hips. Alexis firmly believed Armbruster withheld pertinent information.

The chamber door opened, and Aerianna entered, looking dreadful. Her eyes were red, swollen, and puffy. She wore her red robe, a sign of mourning. Alexis became livid as Aerianna entered the room, wearing the garb.

"Finally, what took you so long?" she hissed, looking at Aerianna. Noticing the red robe, Alexis shook her head with contempt. "How dare you wear the Robe of Tears? Remove it at once. I cannot believe you would do that. Lilah is not dead. She is just missing!"

"My Queen…I simply wanted to honor your feelings of loss and grief during this difficult time. Please accept my apology! Of course, I will change at once."

"No. Hold on, Aerianna. Not so quick," interceded Armbruster. "You are right. We should all be wearing our red robes. We must show the commoners and those around us that this is a difficult time. We must display unity. We should all change our attire at once!" added Armbruster.

Aerianna was shocked. *'Did he just agree with her decision to wear the robe? Wow, that was something new,'* she thought. She bowed down before him respectfully. He placed his hand approvingly on her right shoulder. "Please sit, and let's talk," he demanded.

"Okay, enough already. We will all wear our robes, happy, Armbruster? Can we please get on with it already?" replied a snippy Alexis. She could not understand why there was all this irrelevant chit-chat. *'Why the debate? What a waste of time!'*

"The driver stated it was a woman with astonishing green eyes," relayed Armbruster. He continued, "Also, he indicated he saw strands of her hair from under her hood. He claimed it was jet black. The kidnapper was also very tall. Based on the description, I can only assume it was Lorthana. There is no one else we know matching that exact description. So, the question remains: What do we do next? Shall we transport to Earth to find Lilah? Shall we send a Hunt Team to retrieve Lorthana? How do you wish to proceed, dear?" he asked Alexis, observing her unusually quiet demeanor.

Alexis walked away from the others and headed to the window. She heard enough. Alexis believed it was Lorthana. Angry, she bit her bottom lip, not wanting to yell. Silence filled the room. Trying to regain her composure, she took a deep breath. She would tell them exactly what she wanted them to do.

"I want you to do whatever you must to find that woman. I want her delivered to me in one piece. I want to be the one to put an end to her miserable life if she kidnapped the child. It will be my hands that will drain her life. I want the honor."

Armbruster bowed his head and walked out of the chamber. He was clear on what had to be done. He had no problem with delivering Lorthana to Alexis. If Lorthana were responsible, she would have to pay the price. Alexis would not stand for this betrayal. For once, he agreed with her, though he felt sad. If it were Lorthana, their relationship would end.

Lorthana walked down the narrow corridor of her estate. She carried the *Book of Bartue* in her left hand. She hurried to find Gardone, her husband, and speak with him about Alexis and Armbruster. Lorthana figured Gardone would want to determine where to look next for the pair. She entered his room.

"Hello, dear," she whispered, trying not to disturb him but still get his attention.

"Oh, hello! Come in, Hana," replied Gardone. He always called her Hana, especially when in a good mood.

"What may I do for you? Is that the *Book of Bartue*? Are you still trying to locate them?" he asked, knowing the answer, wondering why Lorthana had not yet given up.

"Gardone, you know I want to find them. I can only assume they are on Alstromia. However, the Globe of Sight is not showing me anything. I have not found them. Zandorah has not heard from them in a long time. She is distraught and annoyed, as well."

"Well, maybe they want to be left alone. They were in quite a hurry to depart Earth. You should respect their wishes. I know you miss her, Hana, but you must let it go. It's only hurting you more every day. She will come to her senses one day and return, I promise."

"You know, dear…What I love most about you is that you are such an optimist. However, I know my daughter. She is headstrong and very stubborn. Well, kind of like her mother. She will not come back here, ever! It breaks my heart as I think of her daily. I cannot even enjoy being a proper Witch here on Earth, knowing my daughter is not here to share all the fun festivities," stated Lorthana.

"Time will heal all of this. Trust me. I must leave you for now and attend a weekly meeting. I will be home later. Please relax and enjoy the full moon." Gardone walked out of the room and into the dark hall with his attendant, Cheeve, right behind him. "Come on, don't walk so slowly. We are going to be late," Gardone reprimanded Cheeve.

On the way out the door, he stopped by the tall shelf to pick up his Ceptre of Stainnard. His father, the Great Warlock Prince Stainnard, passed it down to him after his death.

It was a powerful Ceptre. Its abilities were unknown to most, as it was a secret weapon. However, Gardone knew its power. He was well aware of how it worked and used it to his advantage to resolve issues. With the Ceptre of Stainnard, he was able to locate Alexis and Armbruster the moment they arrived on Alstromia. He knew exactly where they were and did not care.

They were traitors, and like all defectors, they would pay for their abandonment. He walked to Wizzor Hall, where the meeting was scheduled to take place.

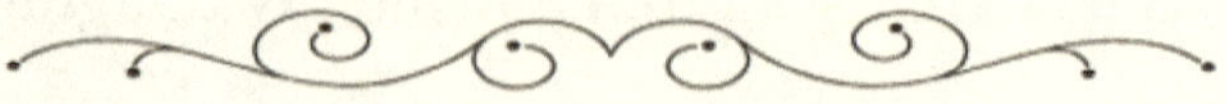

Back on Alstromia, Alexis lounged in her chamber for hours, feeling hopeless and powerless. She desperately wanted her daughter back in her arms. Alexis missed her smile and the adorable, chubby cheeks. She loved her gorgeous, sparkling lavender-colored eyes.

Frustrated, Alexis rose from her chair and marched toward the door. She was about to grab the handle when the door popped open, almost hitting her in the face. "I beg your pardon.... what are you doing? Are you trying to kill me, dumb girl?" she shouted at Carmin.

"Excuse me, Your Royal Highness. I am so sorry. I wanted to know if there was anything I could do for you?" She bowed meekly before the Queen, keeping her head low, showing respect.

"No, there is nothing you can do unless you know where to find my child?"

"No, I am sorry, I do not. I wish I did. May I be excused?" stuttered Carmin.

"By all means, leave!" she dismissed her, waving her hands. At times, she disliked Carmin. *'What a worthless little Witch. She acts more and more like a commoner...no common sense whatsoever!'*

Carmin sprinted from the chamber and headed to her room, crying. She felt miserable, and the Queen continued to make her feel guilty. Carmin had nothing to do with the baby's disappearance and would give her life if it meant getting the Princess back. Lilah captured her heart the moment she met her. Carmin felt responsible for her, and the kidnapping felt personal. She sighed, feeling as if she had failed the Princess.

Once in her room, Carmin closed the thick, velvety curtains and crawled under the blanket, burrowing deeply into the bed. In complete darkness and silence, she cried herself to sleep.

Alexis walked swiftly down the hallway. A few of the workers bowed before her as she passed them. She did not acknowledge them, choosing to keep walking. The Queen was not in the mood to deal with them. '*Commoners,*' she thought!

Armbruster gathered a team in his chamber to deliberate on the urgent need for tighter security. One of the Warlocks suggested the *Chant of Reztec,* a Chant to secure the entire planet. Armbruster already discussed it with Alexis, urging her to allow the group to perform the Chant. It required ten different Warlocks to make it work, and none of them could be from the same Clan.

They needed to be different Guiders. Armbruster liked the idea.

"How many Guiders do we have on Alstromia? Does anyone know?" asked Armbruster, sitting with a group of Wizzards and Warlocks.

"Sir, I believe we have up to twenty-five. However, only eight are in our direct line of command. I suggest interviewing all twenty-five to determine which Guiders can assist us in performing the *Chant of Reztec*. It would be the best plan. Do you think the Queen would help? Her Ceptre is powerful enough to be equal to two or more Guiders. What do you think?" questioned Harshim.

"No, Harshim. I do not want to involve the Queen. She is mourning and not herself. I need you to focus on delivering the twenty-five Guiders to me today. Are you up to the task?"

"Of course, Sir. I will take Samoine with me. He will help. It will take two or more hours... I mean, Mims, but we should be back before evening. I apologize, but I forgot that the Queen does not want us to use Earthly terminology. I apologize. Additionally, I promise not to take up too much time, as I realize we need to expedite this process. Hopefully, we can accomplish it before the morning."

Harshim left the meeting and demanded that his assistant, Samoine, join him. They jumped on two Torrins, pulled back on the reins, and flew off to the City of Miccay to gather the twenty-five Guiders.

Simultaneously, the others silently observed Armbruster, wondering what he was planning. He sat with his right hand against his cheek, tapping his face. He looked deep in thought. Suddenly, the King turned toward the others. His eyes grew big, and his eyebrows raised.

"I have an idea. Let's head to the Carriage stable, speak with Essten, and ask him where his son is hiding. He was not at the stable this morning. I find this very peculiar. We need to make it clear that we must speak with him. Perhaps he saw someone or knows something," announced Armbruster, feeling empowered.

The others nodded their heads in agreement. They concurred. It was odd that Collan was not around. He was always tending to the Torrins, braiding their manes and brushing them. He had been their keeper for years. It seemed highly suspicious that he was missing.

Minutes later, Armbruster approached Essten, looking at him with a frown. Essten was expecting someone to show up to inquire about Collan, but he never thought it would be Armbruster. He bowed and stammered, "Your Royal Majesty…how may I be of assistance? Do you wish to fly one of the Torrins? May I retrieve your favorite one?" he smiled, hoping it would hide his nervousness. A small bead of sweat ran down the left side of his face. He quickly wiped it away.

"We are not here to fly. We are here for Collan! Where is he? He was not here when my security arrived, and they claimed he was missing. So, where exactly is your son, Essten?" Armbruster asked with a tone of interrogation.

"Sir, I have not seen Collan in a while. He did not come to the stable to feed the Torrins today. I arrived early to bring food, and he was not there. My wife informed me he had not been home either. I have no idea where he is at this time. Please accept my apology for his absence. I promise the moment he arrives, I will send him your way," announced Essten nervously. He honestly did not know where Collan was hiding, and he was getting worried. No one had seen him since the day before. It was not like Collan to be gone for long. He loved taking care of the Torrins and took his job seriously.

"Well, that will not do. No, not at all. I want him found now!" He pointed to the house behind the stable. "Search the hut and the grounds. Find him. I want him located immediately. Is that clear?" he barked at the security detail behind him. They nodded in agreement and marched off to start the search.

"Sir, he is not here. I am not lying to you. I have been loyal to you and your family my entire life. I promise! He is missing."

"Essten, I believe you do not know where he is hiding, but we will find him. Let me tell you, if I find out he had anything to do with my daughter's disappearance, he will be sorry. I hope you comprehend what I am saying," he raised his Ceptre and pointed it at Essten as it projected a beam of light. Immediately, Essten felt nauseous. He doubled over in pain and began vomiting. He looked up and wiped his mouth. "Yes, I understand." His entire body felt rubbery. His stomach ached, and his head felt like it was about to explode. He swallowed and tried to keep from vomiting again.

"Good, now go get cleaned up. You look and smell disgusting," Armbruster shouted at Essten. Armbruster lowered his Ceptre. He hated doing that, but he wanted this commoner to understand what he could do to him. That was just a tiny, painful message.

Armbruster felt alive, loving the familiar feeling. Everything was about to change. He refused to back down from the hunt until his daughter was found. The one responsible for the abduction would be held accountable. He would watch them suffer at the hands of his wife, Alexis, and would enjoy watching her destroy the kidnapper.

"Sir, we found this by the back of the hut," Security Guard Porti handed Armbruster a black cloak embroidered with Darbeds. It was saturated with blood and also torn in two areas. Armbruster grimaced as he realized it was a woman's cloak. The robe was also very long, definitely belonging to someone of considerable height. He shook his head. He accepted the cloak from Porti, flung it over his right shoulder, and declared, "I am off to see the Queen. Keep searching. Anything else you find, give to Yarlen. He will ensure I get whatever it is. I want Collan found, is that understood?" asked Armbruster. He was unhappy and keenly aware that Alexis would not like this newly revealed information. He had to find a way to break it to her slowly.

Armbruster decided he would walk back to the Palace to find Alexis. He needed a little time to think about how to inform Alexis about what he had discovered. More than ever, he became convinced that Lorthana had something to do with the audacious kidnapping and feared for her safety.

If Alexis felt her mother was responsible, she would ensure Lorthana would be held accountable for her actions and suffer greatly. He disliked the idea of telling Alexis about his suspicions. Worse, he hated thinking about showing her the cloak. He took it off his shoulder, rolled it into a ball, and carried it behind his back. It would be better if she did not see it right away. He would have to find a way to bring it up and then show it to her. Most likely, there would be little he could do to prepare for the moment. However, he would try to find a way to sneak it into the conversation.

Armbruster entered the Palace and ran into Aerianna in one of the hallways. He asked her if she had any idea where he might find Alexis. She pointed to the balcony, off to the right side of the Hall of Visitation. He thanked Aerianna and approached Alexis, who was standing by the railing. He held the cloak behind his back. Alexis heard him, spun around, and immediately noticed Armbruster's stance. She stared at him with a strange look on her face.

"Umm, what are you hiding from me, Armbruster?" she inquired with piqued curiosity.

"Now, what makes you think I am hiding anything from you?" he smiled nervously, baring his teeth. Armbruster knew what she implied, but was not ready to share the news or show Alexis the cloak.

"I suppose I know you too well. I also see your arm behind your back. Now, why would that be? So, fess up. What is it?" She was already getting annoyed at the game he was playing with her. She knew he had something he wanted to show her, and Alexis assumed it was related to the kidnapping or Lorthana.

"Sit down, Alexis. I need to speak with you." He pointed to the concrete bench.

"No, tell me now! I tire of this game…what is it?"

"Here." He pulled his hand out from behind his back and presented her with the bunched-up cloak. Before he could say anything, she noticed the Darbeds. She could feel the anger rise quickly in her body. She became stiff as she stared at the cloak in disbelief.

"Is that my mother's cloak? Where did you find it? Where is she?" She touched the cloak. "What is that? Is that blood?" She shook her head. A multitude of emotions overwhelmed her all at once. She rubbed her stomach. Alexis cupped her hands over her mouth and glared at Armbruster, feeling ill.

"Yes, it looks like it. It feels and looks like blood. No, I do not know of Lorthana's current whereabouts. I am unsure if it is her cloak. My security detail found it by the stable. I had gone to ask Collan a few questions. Unfortunately, Collan is missing. Essten reported he had been gone for a while."

"Really, and you believed that?" She rolled her eyes at Armbruster skeptically.

"Oh yes…he is telling the truth. I used my Ceptre. He does not know where Collan is, trust me."

"So, what about Marittaz? Does his mother know anything?" Alexis suspected someone was protecting Collan. It probably was Marittaz.

"We could not locate her either. She was not home. My security is also searching for her," added Armbruster, seeing the reaction on Alexis' face. Alexis was not good at disguising her feelings. When she was mad, it was apparent, and currently, she looked furious.

"Marvelous! All the ones we need to speak with are missing. Do you not find this odd? My child is gone, and no one has a clue where she is! I am telling you, someone knows something." Her tone escalated in range, indicating her patience was dwindling quickly.

"Yes, Alexis, someone does know something. We need to find the one that has the correct information. We will locate them soon enough. I have something I am working on right now. I am trying a few new things," Armbruster announced, feeling very sure of himself.

"Trying? Really? Well, that does not make me feel confident in your abilities. Trying is for losers. I need results. Perhaps I should take over this task?" Alexis pointed her Ceptre at him in anger. "You completely amaze me with your *'trying'* comment. I am stunned you would even say that." Alexis was highly disappointed with Armbruster.

"Don't you dare threaten me? You may be Queen, but I am still your husband and leader. Don't you ever forget that! Without me, you would not be Queen. DO YOU GET IT?" he screamed right back at her in anger, his veins bulging out of the sides of his head. His bushy eyebrows were arched high, and his voice was louder than it had been in years.

Alexis backed down. She had not heard him that vocal in a long time. His pure rage made her uncomfortable. At that moment, she feared him. She looked away. *'Hmmm, perhaps there is still hope for Armbruster,'* Alexis thought.

"Yes, I understand." She took the cloak from his hand, left the area, and headed to her chamber. In the hallway, Aerianna took the cloak from her hands and walked silently behind Alexis.

Armbruster paced back and forth, trying to calm down. He had not been that angry or nasty with Alexis in a while. He was frustrated and outraged with her, mostly appalled at her attitude. It was time. He would remind her and the rest of Alstromia that he was still in charge. She was a Queen, a figurehead, but he was the one maintaining control. Things needed to revert to the way they used to be. He needed to dominate her.

Armbruster walked back to his chamber, placing his Ceptre on the shelf. Worried about everything that transpired, he remained silent in the chair by his desk, contemplating his options. Just as he was about to open a book to read, he heard a loud knock on his door.

"Come in," he shouted in an irritated tone.

"Sir, I bring exciting news! I just returned from talking with two of the commoners in the village, and they had some news to share."

"Okay, spit it out! What is it?" asked Armbruster very impatiently.

"Sir, one of the commoners responsible for taking the Torrins back to the building after the arrival of special guests noticed something unusual. He observed that one of the Torrins was not yellow. It was the rare, white kind. It was also not friendly, continually attempting to fly off. The commoner tied the beast up in the dark stable to keep it from getting out. Its owner must have come privately to retrieve it because when he returned later to check on it, it was gone!"

"Really? Well, that is interesting." Armbruster was even more convinced that Lorthana had a part in the kidnapping. His wife's mother was the only owner he personally knew who had a white Torrin. He smiled. *'Finally, a clue worth investigating.'* Armbruster vowed to keep this information private until he knew more. He would withhold all information from Alexis until he had evidence that Lorthana was the one involved with the child's apprehension. If he shared the new information with Alexis too soon, she would most likely jump to conclusions and ruin the investigation. She had to stay out of it for now.

"Thank you. You are dismissed. See Yarlen, and he will reward you."

"Oh, thank you kindly, Sir! I appreciate it." The commoner left the room, eager to locate Yarlen and claim his payment.

Armbruster opened the window for fresh air as he felt suffocated. He flinched, spotting the bright lightning in the sky, and sighed.

The weather made him feel even more glum, and he hated it.

CHAPTER 4

Lorthana placed her favorite cloak at the end of her bed. It was filthy and required washing. She would have Stellah clean it when she finished scrubbing the rest of the estate. She wondered about the status of the hunt for her daughter.

She missed Alexis but was worried that Gardone knew something he was unwilling to share with her. However, she knew better than to question him. The last time she did, he nearly destroyed her. He was not always very loving and, at times, harsh and violent, lacking patience. He adored his daughter, but something evil was in his heart. Lorthana made a point of staying out of his way most of the time.

She gazed out the window and saw smoke billowing out of a chimney from a house down the river. She wondered if the humans knew she lived in the estate on the rugged mountain. Lorthana walked to her messy desk and plopped into the chair. She riffled through a pile of pictures and smiled. Her daughter's picture lay on top. She picked it up and admired her beauty.

"Where are you, my beautiful child? Why did you leave me?" she asked as she started to sob. She wiped away her tears, pretending to act stoic, lovingly gazing at the picture.

The door to her room opened suddenly, and Zandorah appeared. "Hello, Mother!" she shouted.

"My goodness. What are you doing here? When did you arrive?" Lorthana inquired as she walked toward her daughter to embrace her.

Zandorah swiftly pushed her aside. "Enough of the warm hugs and smiles. Mom, I need to speak with you about something quite serious."

"Well, what is it?" asked Lorthana, observing her daughter. She seemed distressed.

"Are we alone? Is Dad around?" Zandorah inspected the room nervously. Lorthana could tell something was wrong.

"No, your father is at the weekly meeting. Why do you ask?" She was beginning to feel a touch uneasy about the line of questioning. "What are you up to, Zandorah?"

"Mom, Lilah is missing, and I know who did it."

"What? What are you saying? Who is Lilah? Why is she missing? What is happening? What are you talking about, Zandi?" asked Lorthana, utterly confused.

"Mom, calm down. Alexis gave birth to a girl—Princess Lilah. They held a ceremony and performed the Ritual of Newcome. That night, Lilah was taken from the Palace on Alstromia, where Alexis and Armbruster reside."

"Okay....and how do you know this information? I have not heard any of this before," screeched Lorthana, frustrated.

"Mom, Dad has known for a while. He told Shawnatar, and Shawnatar informed me. I have no idea why Dad is keeping it a secret. Do you think he had something to do with the disappearance of Lilah?" As she said it, she wanted to retract the statement. She feared her father. He had always been quite powerful, and many Clan members did not trust him. Zandorah had left Earth with Shawnatar for that reason, worried about her safety.

Shawnatar was both her husband's and her father's good friend from the Clan of Tarbo. They had known each other for a while. Though Shawnatar was much younger, they grew powerful together in their magic. The two still communicated and kept each other's secrets. Well, for the most part. Shawnatar did not hide things from Zandorah and believed his wife deserved the truth. So, he disclosed Alexis and Armbruster's location the moment he received the information.

"Why would your father hide this from me? He knows how worried I have been about her absence," asked Lorthana, perturbed.

"Ask him yourself. I have no idea. He is always concealing things. You know this! I am here to share some things with you. For one, Alexis and Armbruster are still on Alstromia, as I previously stated. Two, Lilah is their child. Three, Lilah has been kidnapped and is missing. Four, I know who took her and am fretfully aware they may kill me when they discover what I know. Mom, what should I do?" Zandorah quivered as she spoke, almost stuttering. It was apparent she was terrified. She looked pale, restless, and unable to stay still, walking around while talking with Lorthana.

"Okay, hold on. How did you acquire this information? Who did this evil thing? Tell me, and I will protect you!"

Zandorah laughed hysterically at Lorthana. "What makes you believe for one second you can protect me? You have NO idea who we are dealing with, Mom. Even Dad cannot protect me. Trust me. We are all doomed!"

She threw herself in the chair and began crying. Her long, brown hair fell around her face. Lorthana walked over to her daughter and bent down. She looked up at Zandorah and moved her hair away from her face.

"Zandorah, look at me. It will be okay. Tell me everything you know. Do not leave out anything. I have to know every minuscule detail. I want to help you."

Zandorah gazed deeply into her mother's eyes. She wanted to tell her, but she feared the worst. She looked away, shaking her head repeatedly. Zandorah knew this was a horrible situation, and she hated the fact that she knew so much. It put her life in danger, and those around her as well. Her mother wanted to aid her, but ultimately, her life would be at risk, too. Zandorah was uncomfortable, thinking about the consequences.

"Mom, it was Loggane! He dressed as a woman and kidnapped the Princess. He did it to get back at Alexis. He used your cloak. He stole Pica, your Torrin! He impersonated you! Oh no… We are all dooommmeed." She sobbed loudly, shaking and rocking back and forth with her arms wrapped around her belly.

Lorthana stood up and shook her head, unable to understand why Loggane would kidnap a child. It seemed preposterous that Loggane would believe he could get away with it. Lorthana glanced down at Zandorah. "Get yourself together, child. We must meet with the Clan Witches immediately. Get your cloak, and let's go!"

Lorthana grabbed her green robe from the stand by the desk and quickly threw it on. She zipped it up and made her way to her bookshelf, removing the Staff of Itma. The moment her right hand touched it, the glow became a radiant, bright green. She smiled at Zandorah and raised it high. Both Witches stood side by side. Lorthana slammed the Staff of Itma to the ground, chanting. Green sparks disbursed through the air. The two were enveloped in a neon-green haze and disappeared.

On Alstromia, Armbruster paced up and down the hallway by his chamber. He shuffled his feet, dragging his long cape behind. He twirled his Ceptre around in a circular motion, unaware of the ominous, red light emanating from it. Eventually, the light became very bright. He had to put the Ceptre away to contain its magic. He smiled as he thought about using it to destroy the one who had taken his child.

Quickly, Armbruster's giant grin faded, though. He remembered Alexis making it clear she would be the one to kill the kidnapper. *'So be it,'* he thought. *'Let her do it.'* He would watch with great delight, enjoying the impending torture.

His mood was morose. Aggravated, he walked toward Alexis's chamber. He knew they needed to talk. She had been ignoring him, spending all her time with Aerianna.

The two were most likely plotting something. Alexis had taken the *Book of Aches* into her chamber and ordered Aerianna to research magic to impose the most hurt on the one she would destroy.

Apparently, Alexis was blinded by her hatred and anger. She lost focus and was not thinking about the child. Instead, her entire mission was set to destroy and hurt the one responsible for her child's disappearance. *'How absurd. Why not focus on finding the child first?'* Armbruster became frustrated. Alexis was out of control, and Aerianna only fed into the frenzy!

Armbruster knocked on her chamber door and walked right in without waiting for a reply. Once he opened the door, he found Aerianna sitting beside Alexis, inspecting the book. They both looked up simultaneously as he entered with a scowl.

"Can I help you with something?" Alexis hissed at him.

"My, my, my. What a great way to greet your loving husband," he sarcastically replied.

"What is it you want, Armbruster?" added Aerianna with a self-satisfied expression on her face.

"I am here to speak with my wife. You may leave, Aerianna."

"She most certainly will NOT leave! Stay, Aerianna. Whatever he has to say to me, you can hear," snarled Alexis. She rose from the chair and approached Armbruster.

"What do you want? I have a lot to do, and you are wasting my time. Speak already...." Once standing before him, Alexis observed him with repugnance. She intently stared into his eyes, hoping to make him feel uncomfortable.

"Aerianna, get OUT!" he shouted, raising his Ceptre, hoping to intimidate her.

Aerianna felt uneasy and ran toward the door. " My Queen, I will be back," she yelled as she exited the door. She knew it was best to leave quickly. After all, she did not want to experience Armbruster's wrath.

"Do you feel better now? Why did you have to do that? You are downright rude." Infuriated, Alexis rolled her eyes at Armbruster. She despised his lack of control and quick temper.

"Silence! I have something to tell you. Not everything we discuss concerns your best friend. Now, shut your mouth and listen for once," he demanded. He shook his head, looking Alexis straight in the face. She had a way of bringing out the worst in him. He hated it because it made him feel less in control. Alexis was a great manipulator. She knew how to push his buttons and took pleasure in watching his reactions.

Alexis walked to the fireplace and sat down reluctantly in the oversized chair. She squinted her eyes, glaring at him with anger. "Fine, say what you must," she sarcastically responded, knowing she had upset him.

"Alexis, my security team received word that Zandorah knows we are on Alstromia. Also, your father called a weekly meeting to discuss our disappearance from Earth. I know this because I have spies on Earth to help protect us. Zandorah is supposedly also aware of who took Lilah. She is meeting with Lorthana as we speak. I think we should bring Zandorah here. She is not safe on Earth!"

"So... my sister knows who did this? Why are you not on Earth, retrieving and questioning her? For all we know, she had something to do with it," retorted Alexis.

"I do not believe she had anything to do with the kidnapping. She claims to know who did it. Her life is in danger. Shawnatar is in danger, too. I know you may not care for Zandorah's welfare, but I know you care about what happens to Shawnatar," he murmured, making eye contact with Alexis. He knew, without a doubt, that the statement would make her change her mind. He believed Alexis still had feelings for Shawnatar after all this time. If anything, she would request Shawnatar's presence on Alstromia. She would not allow the love of her life to be in danger.

Zandorah was a different story. Alexis would have mixed feelings about her sister's safety. Their relationship was strained over

Shawnatar, neither wanting to fix nor discuss the situation. They were both extremely stubborn.

Alexis turned her head away from Armbruster, focusing on the flames of the fire. Sitting next to the fireplace, she felt warm but shivered. Thinking about Shawnatar brought back all sorts of memories and emotions. He was the one she had loved more than life itself, only to be taken from her by Zandorah. She would never forgive her sister for the betrayal! Yes, Armbruster was correct. She cared for Shawnatar and would want him here. She wanted him safe, even if Zandorah wasn't. It did not matter to her what happened to Zandorah. She betrayed her, and their sisterly love was no more.

"Send out a Hunt Team to retrieve them from Earth. I want them here, and I demand answers," she growled. Armbruster decided to approach Alexis to console her, but she merely brushed him away. "Go on, get it done! Do what you do best. Leave!"

Feeling defeated, Armbruster walked toward the door. He turned around to watch Alexis by the window, knowing Shawnatar was on her mind, her one true love. Armbruster had always known there was no way he could compete. Sadly, he stopped trying a long time ago. For now, he would deal with Shawnatar's presence once again. Armbruster despised the idea. However, he knew it was out of his control. Alexis ordered his presence, and so it would happen.

Armbruster left Alexis alone, walking in the direction of his chamber. Halfway there, he saw Aerianna talking with Tamarah, one of the older Clan Witches. He stopped to say hello, hoping to hear what they were discussing. Tamarah smiled sweetly and excused herself as soon as she saw Armbruster's approach. Aerianna glared at Armbruster. Her head tilted to the side.

"What? Is there something else I can do for you?" She looked at him with hatred.

"Yes, as a matter of fact, there is. You can take care of my wife. She is not well. Protect her and be there for her. Act like her friend. For once, stop thinking about yourself."

Armbruster walked off without saying another word. He made his point. She annoyed him so much, and he wished she had not come to live in the Palace. Aerianna was becoming too much like Alexis, which was problematic.

Aerianna watched Armbruster walk down the hall and wondered what was happening. She planned to find out. She would ask Alexis the instant she saw her.

Armbruster was becoming too vocal and much too snippy for her liking.

Aerianna entered Alexis' chamber in a huff. She felt perturbed about her quick, one-sided conversation with Armbruster. As she neared Alexis, she could tell she had been crying a lot. Her eyes were swollen and red. Her face was wet from tears. She looked dreadful. Her hair was messy and sticking to her cheek.

"What may I do for you, my friend?" she asked Alexis, observing her.

"Did you know, Zandorah and Shawnatar are aware we are here? Did you also know they are on their way to Alstromia? Armbruster is assembling a Hunt Team to deliver them to me. Supposedly, Zandorah knows who took my precious little girl. She will have no choice but to tell me. Trust me. I will not allow her to lie. I will not tolerate her dishonesty or complete disregard for my feelings." Alexis threw a cup at the wall and watched it shatter into pieces. She was enraged at the thought that her sister was hiding information from her. '*How dare Zandorah keep secrets from me,*' she thought.

Aerianna approached the broken glass, bent down, and cleaned it up. "Don't touch it. I will have someone else take care of it. I do not want you performing menial jobs."

Alexis yelled for Karita, one of the commoners. She quickly entered the chamber, removed the broken glass as ordered, and hastily left the room.

Alexis and Aerianna sat alone in the chamber. Thunder boomed outside, causing the massive window in the room to rattle. The only other noise to be heard was the crackling of the fire in the fireplace. Finally, after a few minutes, Aerianna spoke up.

"What do you want to do, Alexis? Do you have a plan? Is there anything I can assist you with at this time? I know you are bitterly upset!"

"No, there is nothing you can do. We must wait to see if Armbruster can retrieve them from Earth. I can tell you with certainty that I am getting more impatient. It has been almost a day since my precious child was taken from me. None of the spells reveal her location. This is so odd. Someone must have cast a *Concealment Spell*. Even Armbruster stated it is unusual, and he usually knows everything. He instructed Yarlen to use his Ceptre as Head Seeier to find Lilah. Yet, he found nothing. I am beyond anxious."

Alexis walked to her bed and threw herself on top, her feet dangling off the edge. She lay on her back, staring at the ceiling, not knowing if she wanted to scream or cry. She folded her arms and continued to look up.

Nothing made sense to her. The situation was out of control. Alexis did not like the feeling. It evoked too much anger.

Armbruster burst through the door with Yarlen. Alexis sat up quickly, puzzled. "What is it?" she immediately asked.

"They found Shawnatar but not Zandorah. Your mother, Lorthana, is gone too. No one knows where they are hiding. Your father is at home, waiting for their arrival. He promised he would let me know when they returned. I think we need to prepare for anything at this point. I am deathly afraid something awful is happening directly involving Lorthana and Zandorah. Unfortunately, I have no idea what. Yarlen, did you manage to see anything?" Armbruster spun around, facing his Second-in-Command, hoping the old Wizzard had good news to share.

"No, Your Majesty. My Ceptre is unable to shed light on the situation. It is as if the Princess simply vanished. She is nowhere." He shook his head in disbelief and anger. Yarlen did not like informing Alexis and Armbruster that he could not *'see'* the child. After all, it was his responsibility and job as Head Seeier to see everything and provide valuable information.

Something was wrong. His powers were not working. No matter what he did, no matter what he tried, nothing was revealed. Yarlen felt useless, and it made him frustrated. He did not want the Queen or Armbruster to blame him for his inability to find the child.

"I was just explaining to Aerianna that I believe there is a *Concealment Spell* over all of this. Otherwise, we would have some kind of revelation," added Alexis. She looked proud, as if she was adding something of value to their conversation.

"I agree. However, you know, as well as the rest of us, reversing such magic is virtually impossible. Yarlen, where do we stand with the *Chant of Reztec*? Have we managed to find the required Guiders to perform the Chant?" questioned Armbruster, observing his friend. Yarlen was quick to respond.

"No, we found eight, but that is not enough. I will speak with the remaining Guiders and determine what we can do. I shall return as quickly as I can. I am at a loss as to why we have been unable to locate enough Guiders." Yarlen hastily left the chambers and headed to the Hall.

Armbruster and Alexis were losing their patience with the entire process. It was taking too long. Alexis was not an easy-going Witch and would not allow this situation to continue forever. She liked structure and planning. Nothing so far had been planned well. Likely, she would eventually take things into her own hands. Alexis would involve Aerianna because she was just like her: power-hungry and driven. The circumstances would only worsen. The old Wizzard knew it was up to him and Armbruster to find a way to diffuse the situation and locate the missing child.

"What do you want to do, Alexis? I have done everything that I can. I believe I will retire to my chamber and hopefully sleep. I am beyond exhausted. You should do the same. Do you want me to stay and keep you company?" Armbruster asked Alexis, knowing the answer in advance. She would not allow him to stay.

"No, I wish to be alone. I will attempt to figure it all out. I have much to consider. Thank you, though." Alexis realized Armbruster had tried. Unfortunately, he failed. Armbruster always failed her when she needed him the most. She stopped relying on him a long time ago. Alexis simply pretended to ask for his assistance, to keep him believing she still trusted him, even though she did not.

Alexis knew he was incapable of being the Warlock he had once been. He lost credibility among the Clan and turned soft. She wished he would regain his stamina and become the Warlock she fell in love with—strong, powerful, and relentless.

Armbruster's eyes caught Aerianna giving him a dirty look. He felt disgusted, wishing she would return to Earth and stay far away from his wife. Aerianna was always there, right next to the Queen. He was never allowed to be near Alexis anymore. It was an outrage. He stormed out of the room and slammed the door. Enraged, he changed his mind about sleeping. It would be better to join Yarlen and the other Guiders in the Hall of Visitation.

Aerianna rolled her eyes, furious with Armbruster over his obnoxious behavior. *'Why did he have to be so mean all the time? The nerve of him. He is making everything more difficult for Alexis. Does he not understand Alexis is already upset? She does not deserve Armbruster's lack of self-control.'* Aerianna took the book off the desk and tucked it under her arm. She turned around and stood by the chamber door.

"Alexis, I hope you get some rest. I will look through the book for new spells. There must be something we can do. I will also meet with Farla to ascertain if she has any suggestions. After all, she is the one with the most knowledge of spellcraft. I promise we will find something, Alexis." She gave her a pretend smile and left the room, leaving

Alexis to think. Aerianna held the book close to her body as she strolled along the dimly lit corridor.

Her heart raced as she thought about Farla. Many feared her because she was audacious, resourceful, and masterful in her craft. However, Aerianna realized they needed her assistance. Farla was possibly the only one capable of counteracting the *Spell of Concealment*. She was a stellar Witch. Most thought she was a bit eccentric. She was short, stout, rather mouthy, and not the kindest of Witches. However, no one could deny she was more gifted than most. Thus, many kept their opinions about Farla to themselves.

Armbruster entered the Hall of Visitation and joined the group of Guiders. Several had great advice to share, but none knew what to do. Yarlen looked pale. His usual flushed cheeks looked ashen. His hair was neither tidy nor pulled back into its usual ponytail. Instead, it looked wild and messy. Apparently, he was not handling the situation well. Perhaps he felt blamed for not seeing anything, thereby being unable to aid the King and Queen. Possibly, it was a massive weight of guilt on his shoulders.

Yarlen slumped in the wooden chair, reflecting his negative mood.

"Guiders, please be quiet. We must pull together. We currently have eight Guiders to assist with performing the Chant. This is fantastic news. We only require two more. I believe there are two other Guilders in the next village over. One of you will need to head there tonight to find them. Arlow and Camrun are capable Guilders, and we could use their assistance. They will be ready to aid us if we ask them. The Chant must be performed by the end of the night. So, hurry. Bring them back immediately," ordered Armbruster.

"Yes, Your Majesty. I will take a Torrin and leave now," replied Hamptin.

"Excellent. You are a true friend and the most valuable Guider. Thank you. Please, be safe!" responded Armbruster. He was happy to see Hamptin stand up. At times, he was a bit on the shy side and not too forceful, though he was a very talented Guider.

The remaining Guiders stayed in the room, planning the night's event. The *Chant of Reztec* was extremely complex, requiring specific magical items to make the incantation effective. All necessary articles were held in the Tower, a storage facility in the Palace. Only those authorized could enter this high-security area, and Armbruster elected to retrieve the supplies himself.

"Yarlen, will you assist me in collecting the goods? I could use your help," requested Armbruster. He handed Yarlen an enormous black bag from the table, a magical Chant Bag. The bag was deep and capable of holding heavy items. It was constructed from the inside of Trimbers, which is known for its durability and hardness. This part of the Trimbers was often used to make bags or boxes and was woven for additional strength. Yarlen took the Chant Bag and flung it over his right shoulder. The two Wizzards left the Hall and walked toward the Tower at the other end of the Palace. Outside the room, however, Yarlen stopped.

"Sir, there is something I have to tell you. You will not be happy about what I must share with you. I apologize in advance. I'm sorry," Yarlen confessed in a high-pitched and squeaky voice.

"Well, what is it? Tell me. You know I trust you."

"My son, Garlow, saw one of them—the evil ones, who took the Princess. He was too scared to tell you. He was worried you would think he had something to do with it. He departed for Earth to find them."

"What are you saying? Are you telling me he knows who did this?"

"He believes it was Loggane—your sister's son, your nephew. I did not want to say anything until we knew for sure. I am sorry I kept it from you. I just wanted to ensure the facts were correct before notifying you. Now, I believe you need to know, no matter what." Nervously, Yarlen continued walking, hoping Armbruster would take the news well.

"You did the right thing by telling me. I am not mad. I am taken aback by the fact that you did not tell me before. Do not worry about it. I believe you. I know you are always an ally. Your intentions are well known, and I trust you with the well-being of my family. Honestly, if I did not trust you, you would not be here." Armbruster put his hand on Yarlen's shoulder. He was not angry, simply annoyed by the whole situation. The two continued their walk toward the Tower. Neither spoke.

Meanwhile, Alexis was dressed in a long and comfortable sleeping gown. She brushed her hair while taking swigs of her Brew potion. She placed the glass on the table beside her bed for easy access. She called Karita to tend to the fire. She could have used magic, but it was more enjoyable to make Karita work. She was lazy, and Alexis felt the girl needed to earn her keep. Karita, a tiny commoner, came to work for her a long time ago. Essten highly recommended her to Alexis.

When Alexis first met Karita, she acted nervously, accidentally spilling a drink on Alexis. Karita assumed she would not be offered the job. However, Alexis surprised her by giving her the position anyway. Alexis thought the girl handled herself well despite her clumsiness. Karita did not display intelligence, which Alexis thought was a bonus. It would not be difficult to keep her out of her business.

Once the fire roared, Alexis crawled into her bed and drew the covers up to her chin. She watched the fire from her bed and thought about Lilah. Tears started to flow from her big, green eyes and ran down her cheeks. She began to sob, her heart aching. All she wanted was to have Lilah back in her arms, safe and sound. How could she go on without her? Would she ever see her little Princess again? Her head hurt severely, and stabbing pains in her skull made her nauseous. Alexis closed her eyes, trying desperately to think about other things. Slowly, she drifted off to sleep, still slightly sobbing, holding on to Lilah's favorite toy—a little brown, fuzzy bunny. It was a gift from her friend Shell.

Arriving on Earth, Lorthana and Zandorah popped into the Chant Chamber in the Hall of Wizdom, known to be the most powerful place for Witches on Earth. The cylinder-shaped building was constructed of aging, irregularly shaped blocks. It was covered in moss and ivy, blending inconspicuously into the woodsy scenery. Inside the building, the entry was large and bare. A massive stone staircase led to the basement and the Chant Chamber. Lorthana placed her Ceptre behind her back and walked toward the Chant Circle to join the others. Each Witch placed their Staff or Ceptre outside the circle one by one. They sat on the gigantic red pillows, avoiding the painted, peeling, and cold concrete floor.

"Clan Witches, I need your immediate support. As some of you may know, my daughter, Alexis, and her husband, Armbruster, departed Earth to live on another planet. She recently gave birth to her first child, Princess Lilah. The baby was kidnapped on the night of her welcoming and the Ritual of Newcome! Zandorah, my other daughter, is here with me today. We seek your assistance to keep the forces away that try to destroy us. We need your help and magical abilities. Please, let me explain further," announced Lorthana, surveying the attentive group.

Lorthana spent quite some time explaining the entire circumstance to the Clan Witches. After she finished speaking, the room became hushed. Nervous Clan members looked around, unsure how to respond. No one wanted to be the first one to speak up.

"So, what exactly do you need from us, Lorthana? I understand you need protection, but what are we to do?" asked Chynah, a red-haired Clan Witch. She smiled but appeared perplexed.

"Yes, we can help cast spells. However, some spells will work on Earth's inhabitants, who are primarily humans. Weak Witches, Warlocks, and Wizzards may be targeted. What specifically are you asking us to do?" chimed in Starlitte. She was a tiny and young Clan Witch with excellent protection spell abilities. It was her greatest strength.

"I am asking for any assistance to keep Zandorah safe. As I stated, she is in danger. Until we find the one who kidnapped my granddaughter, Zandorah is in danger. I hope we can unite and become a powerful force against this evil. I humbly ask you to join me in any way you can." Lorthana stood up and walked to the oval table by the fireplace. She placed her Ceptre sideways, facing the Clan. "I am at a loss. You know I am not a mean Witch, but I am more than willing to be aggressive if necessary. My daughter's life depends on it. I have not yet met my grandchild. Can you imagine? Some of you are aware of how protective I am of those I love. I will fight until the end to protect my family. Can I count on you?" she boldly asked, making eye contact with the crowd.

She waited for a response, releasing a huge sigh. It did not take long. The Witches quickly approached and protectively encircled Lorthana and Zandorah. Lorthana and her daughter stood in silence while the rest of the Clan Witches chanted their protection spells. Once complete, everyone smiled, feeling a sense of relief. It was a moment of reassurance. They were safe, though possibly just for a while. Hopefully, the Chant had worked well enough.

Not far away, a small group of Warlocks met in a candlelit room. One of the Warlocks wore a green cape, with only his eyes visible. He smiled under his cloak, knowing soon he would have what he wanted. There was no doubt that Alexis would pay for her betrayal. He was tired of waiting. Now was the time! He glanced down at the tiny child in the wooden crate. She looked beautiful, and he could not help but see Alexis in her. Yes, the Queen was definitely the mother of this child. She would never see this baby again as long as he was in control!

He walked to the next room to meet with the other Warlocks to discuss their plan's next step. It was a brilliant and well-thought-out strategy to take back power. He was about to regain control. It was just a matter of time. Now that he had what Alexis wanted more than anything, he knew she would negotiate. He had no doubt. His smile widened as he thought about his impending victory.

CHAPTER 5

Shawnatar sat quietly at the table, looking through various old, dusty books. He could not believe Zandorah had just left like that without any notice. '*What is she thinking?*' He thought about Armbruster and the fact that he probably told Alexis everything they had hidden from her.

Presumably, she was aggravated by now. Shawnatar missed watching her eyes widen right before she laughed or screamed. He missed her pouty smile. Well, he just missed Alexis, though he learned to live without her. Shawnatar told himself he loved Zandorah. It was easier this way for everyone. Yes, he was a good friend to all, or so he wanted to convince himself.

Shawnatar shoved one of the books off the table, and it landed on the floor with a thud. He was miserable, forcing himself to forget about Alexis for years. Now, she had a child, though not his. It was Armbruster's child, his best friend's. It was difficult for him to accept. Suddenly, he felt enormous guilt. *'Was it my fault the baby was kidnapped? Is it someone I know? Perhaps someone knows about my feelings for Alexis?'* Did any of it have to do with him, or perhaps Zandorah? He had so many questions.

Still angry, Shawnatar stood before the fireplace and threw a book onto the flames. He watched it catch fire and burn. He wondered why it made him feel better, laughing out loud, alone, in the room. He snatched his Chant Robe from a chair and headed to the next room to meet with the other Warlocks. He wanted to ensure everything was done to protect Alexis and Zandorah. He also realized the Princess had to be found quickly. These were difficult circumstances.

Somehow, Shawnatar knew things would work out. However, he feared someone else would be hurt before all was done. He was terrified at the thought that it could be Zandorah. He pushed the idea out of his head as he opened the door to the Meeting Room. It took only a second. The pain hurt so great. He closed his eyes as he fell onto the hard, dirty concrete floor.

As his eyes fluttered about to close, he looked up briefly and saw him! Loggane smiled down at him with a wicked grin. His statuesque and muscular body towered over Shawnatar, looking smug. His bold, blue eyes danced with delight as he watched Shawnatar pass out. It was the last thing Shawnatar remembered before becoming unconscious.

"Someone move him to the large sofa over there," Loggane pointed to the long, brown couch by the wall. "Hurry up. I want him tied up. I do not want him to get away," ordered Loggane.

"Sir, I am not sure he is still alive. He is bleeding profusely. What should we do? Shall we fix him manually or perform a spell?" asked Markis as he watched the blood running off Shawnatar's head, dripping onto the floor.

"Check on him and keep him alive. I need him. Do whatever it takes."

Loggane gazed down at Shawnatar, sprawled out on the couch. *'He looks okay. Why is Markis worried? A little blood never hurt anyone. He is a Warlock. It isn't like he will die so quickly. He is still breathing,'* Loggane rationalized. He could not help but feel happy as he looked at the vulnerable being, passed out, not able to do a thing to defend himself.

"I am off to find the book in the attic. Get him cleaned up and put him in a new robe. He looks vile. I despise the sight of blood. Clean it up," growled Loggane. He stormed out of the room and headed to the attic, ready to search the library for the elusive book. Loggane realized there was a slim chance he would find it. Nonetheless, he planned to try.

Not too long ago, he had discovered the missing *Spell of Concealment* in an ancient book. Everyone believed it was destroyed. It had been his most precious discovery to date. He was proud of himself and wanted to search the library for other potentially powerful spells. Little did anyone know he had many ancient books containing powerful chants and spells stored in the attic. He could use them as needed. A huge grin covered his face, thinking about what he could unleash upon others. Spell power was a great gift, and he planned to use it considerably.

Loggane entered the makeshift library in the attic, which was cold and dark. There were no windows or other exits. A single rusty metal door allowed entry into the stagnant room, permeated with a moldy smell. The room was filled with a vast number of books. Some were very old, brittle, and in a state of disrepair. The shelves, made of wood, bowed from the heavy weight of the books.

The library was neglected and dirty, coated with dust, and full of Cuvvey webs, courtesy of a Cuvvey, an earthly-looking spider. Gigantic piles of papers lined an entire wall, stacked from floor to ceiling. Loggane had not attempted to scour through the mountain of papers. He wondered if the documents were someone's notes. If so, they could be potentially worthless information.

He walked from bookshelf to bookshelf, seeking the mysterious and missing book. *'Where is the black book with silver print?'* He remembered seeing it a while back. He was sure it was here, somewhere. It could not just have disappeared.

Perplexed, he decided to check out the boxes in the corner and dug through them. He previously tried to use his magic to locate the book but was unsuccessful. It was bizarre. None of the spells seemed to work. *'Why is my magic not working? Is someone blocking my abilities?'* He became livid.

Loggane continued to scour through boxes and shelves frantically. He was unable to locate the item he was looking for. *'Where is the book?'* Just as he was about to give up, he came across an interesting book. It was bright red, with bold, gold-embossed letters and a frayed edge. The text read: *Enchantment. 'A simple but intriguing title,'* he thought.

He sat down on a nearby stool and flipped open the large book. Examining the various chapters, he realized the pages were still legible. One of the chapters caught his attention—*Concealment!* He flipped to Chapter 9. He ran his crooked, long finger down the page until he found the word: *Suppression.* Instantly, he grinned from ear to ear. *'Victory!'*

Shawnatar tried to open his eyes, though his head pounded. An annoying screeching noise in his ears made him violently nauseous. Bravely, he forced himself to open his eyes.

Slowly, he opened them, attempting to squint just enough to see. He spotted a fireplace, though it was blurry. He could faintly hear voices, possibly emanating from another room. He struggled to move but felt tied down. Frustrated, he looked ahead, attempting to survey his surroundings. It became clear to him. He was still in the same building as before. He wondered, *'What happened? Did I see Loggane? What is going on?'* Shawnatar attempted to sit up. With much effort, he eventually managed to do so. Instantly, his head pounded louder than before.

Boom… Boom… Boom… thunderous noise in his head, aching. His head felt as if it was splitting in half. He licked his lips and tasted iron, realizing it was blood. Nervously, he swallowed hard, trying to stay focused, though it was difficult.

Quickly, he discovered he was tied up and could not move. He could not stand up without falling. Shawnatar sat quietly, straining to think. It was proving challenging, given the massive headache.

Suddenly, things became clearer. Shawnatar recalled dressing in his cloak, walking into a room, and then experiencing a substantial hit on the head. Next, he saw Loggane's face—the evil grin, smiling down at him. *'What occurred?'* Just as he was about to yell for help, he heard two voices getting louder as if they were approaching. He decided to lie back down and pretend to be knocked out. He slowed his breathing and closed his eyes.

"Seems like Prince Charming is still sleeping," noted Adoren. He smirked as he inspected Shawnatar. "What a fool. I am so glad Loggane is taking care of all the weaklings."

"Yes, we certainly do not need anyone in our Clan who cannot or does not want to help Loggane regain power. Worthless...," growled Bartin as he stared at Shawnatar's body. Bartin touched Shawnatar's forehead. "He is getting a bit hot. Do you think he is okay? Loggane does not want him dead. What should we do?"

"Leave him. He will be fine. We must retrieve the potion from the Witch. It should be ready by now. We do not want to upset Loggane again. This insignificant being is securely tied up and not going anywhere."

"Okay, if you think so. Let's head out."

The two Warlocks left the chamber. The moment they were gone, Shawnatar forced himself to sit up. Again, the familiar pounding in his head. His vision remained blurry. He scoured the room for weapons. A glistening object near the table caught his attention.

Shawnatar dropped onto the floor and crawled toward it. He looked up at the table to see a long dagger with a strange twisted handle. Shawnatar tried to grab it with his mouth since his hands were still bound. It took him four tries, but eventually, he managed to hold onto it between his teeth.

Strategically, Shawnatar released it, dropping it close to his body. He would try to grab it with one of his hands. It did not take long. Once he held it securely in his right hand, he moved it back and forth to cut the ties around his wrists. Success! He was free. Next, he cut through the leg ties. Once he managed to untie himself, he stood up.

Immediately, he noticed his legs felt weak and shaky. He stumbled toward the couch to rest. *'What can I do?'* He noticed something odd. Worried, he reached up and placed his hand on the top of his skull. Instantly, he felt warm wetness. He pulled his hand away and saw dark, red blood.

Nervously, he grabbed the cloak from a chair near the fireplace. He placed it on his head, hoping to absorb the blood.

After some time, it seemed as if the bleeding stopped. Shawnatar returned to the couch and took the ties he had previously removed from his hands and feet. He tossed them and the blood-soaked cloak into the fireplace. *'No need to leave evidence behind,'* he thought. He managed to make his way to the tall, wooden door. Apprehensively, he propped his head up against it to listen. Since he heard nothing, he believed escaping was safe.

Cautiously, he opened the door, peering around the corner to look for others. He saw no one. He entered the hallway, looking down both ways. *'Which way to go?'* He walked as quickly as he could, heading toward the end of the building. He exited in a hurry, though his legs felt like rubber.

Upstairs in the attic, Loggane smirked. He figured out his next step. He also realized it would require more help. Undeniably, he would take the lead but needed others' assistance, though he disliked the idea of asking anyone for help.

Loggane placed the book inside his cloak's large side pocket and headed down the stairs. He proceeded toward the large chamber. Opening the door, he instantly noticed something was wrong.

' Where is Shawnatar? Where are the idiots, Bartin and Adoren? They were supposed to be watching him.' Loggane became enraged. *'If they took him, they will DIE! If Shawnatar got away on his own, they will DIE…either way, they will DIE!'* His forehead scrunched in anger. He violently slammed down his heavy Ceptre and disappeared.

In the Palace, Alexis glared at Aerianna, waiting for a reply. "Well, what do you think?" she asked, demanding an answer. Her impatience was obvious.

"Well, I believe it does not make a difference what I think. What matters is that you are happy with the decision."

"Listen, I did not assign you as my Second-in-Command to have you act indecisively. Make up your mind and say so. I am not in the mood for any kind of game. You either give me your opinion, or there is no need for you to continue being my Second-in-Command," yelled Alexis, making her point.

"Alexis, I only meant…you need to do what you feel is appropriate. It is not up to me to tell you what to do."

"If I wanted someone weak and wavering, I could have made Armbruster my Second-in-Command. I placed you in the position because you have always provided your opinion. Why change now? I must tell you, I do not like this side of you," Alexis walked to the fireplace and turned her back to Aerianna. Fuming, she crossed her arms and tapped her right foot.

"Very well, then. I will share my feelings with you." Aerianna took a deep breath. Alexis spun around quickly, facing Aerianna. "I think it is a great plan. I also believe it will showcase your capabilities and make it clear that you will not accept anything other than their complete loyalty. You will need to act quickly, though. Armbruster is trying to gain support. I believe he is attempting to overthrow your power."

"WHAT? Are you sure?" Alexis asked. The idea that Armbruster had the audacity to do something so underhanded enraged her.

"I am quite sure. Your loving husband suddenly wants to be in charge again. He is meeting and talking with Warlocks about changes. You need to be careful, Alexis. He will betray you."

"Aerianna, watch what you say! You are accusing my husband of treason and are implying a coup."

"Your Royal Highness, I am very well aware of what I am saying and realize the consequences of my words. However, I vowed to protect you and this planet. I have many spies. I received information that Armbruster is doing many things, mostly aimed at regaining power."

"That underhanded, traitorous, back-stabbing liar. I need immediate proof, Aerianna. We must put a stop to his actions immediately. Given all that has happened recently, this is what he is most concerned about right now. Unbelievable! I tell you what... he will be sorry he did this. Armbruster will regret his actions until the last breath of his existence."

Alexis raised her Ceptre, closed her eyes, and slammed down the Star Ceptre as she chanted. She vanished into a grey fog, leaving Aerianna stupefied. For a moment, Aerianna felt upset, but then a sinister smile surfaced on her face. Her plan had worked perfectly. Everything would change now. She was elated at the prospect of causing a rift between Alexis and Armbruster. When all was said and done, she wanted to be next to Alexis, not Armbruster. Aerianna left to head to her chamber, ready to figure out what to do next.

Not far away, in another chamber, Armbruster listened attentively as he heard a tale that made his stomach ache. So much betrayal, so many lies. *'Why? For What?'* He shook his head. *'Can I trust anyone?'*

Yarlen observed Armbruster and sympathized with him. He could only imagine how he felt. The King's wife betrayed him like that. *'Horrible,'* thought Yarlen. He nervously glanced at Armbruster, who stood up and paced back and forth, shaking his right fist.

"Are you sure?" Armbruster repeatedly asked Porti.

"Yes, Sir! I am positive. I heard it myself. She is planning to do it by tonight. Well, she was... before the child was taken. I do not know if she changed the plans for the night or not. She might postpone it now. Sorry, it's difficult to be certain at this point. So much has transpired," Porti replied.

"I want you to bring Aerianna to me. I need her alive so we can interrogate her. Do you understand, Porti?"

"Yes, Your Majesty. It shall be done." Porti ordered his guards to accompany him as he set out to retrieve Aerianna. He knew it would be a challenge. She would not come quietly nor willingly, probably using magic to evade them. They would need to be prepared and bring the Mesmer Ceptres.

"Sir, are you sure we can trust Porti?" asked Yarlen apprehensively.

"Without a doubt. Porti has always been loyal. He would not lie."

"No offense, Sir, but many have betrayed you recently. How do we know who we can trust?"

"I cast a *Respect Spell* when he began sharing the details. It was the only way I could ensure his honesty."

"Very clever! It's no wonder you're such a great leader. You're always ahead of the game."

"Sadly, not this time. I was totally unaware of her lies and deceit. I cannot believe Alexis planned to have me removed from my position. Who does she think she is? I have too many powerful friends and Warlocks on my side. She does not stand a chance. Alexis lost her mind!"

"Perhaps it was the childbirth? Do you think it is what made her this way?" Yarlen questioned, hoping for a reaction from Armbruster.

"No, she has always been this way. Now, she is just power-hungry. She believes that I stand in her way since I will not allow her to run me or do harmful things. That is why she wants me out of the way. I am sure she knows I would not go willingly. Her actions deeply hurt me: my beautiful wife, a treasonous Witch. I must put a stop to this once and for all. I always felt this new leadership idea was an irrational one. I should not have agreed. I wanted to please her and make her happy. Look what I did. I created a monster." Armbruster appeared defeated, with tears in his eyes.

The loud pounding knock on the chamber door interrupted Armbruster's thoughts.

"Come in," he shouted, still exasperated.

"Sir, we have found Collan," the security officer announced.

"That is great news. Bring him to me immediately!"

"Sir, he is dead!"

"What? Dead? Tell me what happened," commanded Armbruster.

"Sir, they discovered him floating in the River of Miccay. He…well, he is dead. Let's leave it at that."

"I want to see him. Bring him here to the Palace at once!"

"Yes, Your Majesty. We will do so immediately. I will notify you once he is in Visitation Hall."

"Fine, you do that," grumbled Armbruster.

"What do you think about that, Yarlen? How did this happen to Collan? Who did this to the poor boy?"

"Sir, I guess it has something to do with the Queen. I am in no way trying to be disrespectful, but perhaps it is because of the implementation of her new plan."

"You are correct. Alexis is undoubtedly responsible. I sure would like to know why. I should confront her and ask."

"Sir, I do not believe that is a good idea. We should not let her know we are on to her plans."

"Once again, Yarlen, you are very wise. Thank you for thinking clearly when I struggle to do so. My mind is confused. I miss my child. I am horrified by my wife's actions and worried about Zandorah and Shawnatar."

"Sir, why don't you try to rest? I promise to inform you the minute they deliver Collan's body to the Palace. Shall I notify Essten?"

"No, absolutely not. Essten has been a loyal worker and friend. I will tell him later. Much later, after I rest a bit. Inform the others that no one is to say a word about Collan's death. Is that clear?"

"Yes, Your Majesty. I understand and shall obey. I will ensure you are the one to announce Collan's death." Yarlen left the chamber and headed to his room. He wished to research spells that could be used on Alexis if things turned out worse than anticipated. Yarlen felt somber. This entire mess with Alexis could cause an outright war on Alstromia. He knew this was all part of her plan to undermine Armbruster's leadership and subsequently gain complete control over all of Alstromia. Technically, as Queen, she held that power, but many still looked to Armbruster. Alexis despised that fact and planned to show others she was the only one in charge of Alstromia.

Armbruster headed to his private chamber. There, he sat on his bed, peering out the window. Rain poured out of the sky. He loathed the rain. The thought depressed him further. He missed the sunshine and warmth on his face, wishing he were back on

Earth with his friends. He loved and preferred the smells there, adoring the planet's four changing seasons. He realized for the first time that he genuinely hated Alstromia. Alexis ruined everything. *'Why is she doing this? Why can't things stay the same? She never has enough power. Alexis needs power to be happy.'* He realized long ago that she would do whatever it took to get and maintain it. Armbruster understood what happened. He lost his child and his wife in one swift move. Feeling angry, he closed his eyes. Sleep was the only thing he wanted. He did not wish to think about anything else.

In the brightly illuminated chamber, Yarlen opened the large, golden book. He flipped through the pages, looking for something in particular. He scratched his head and retied the ribbon, holding his hair in place. His beard itched. Everything annoyed him as he struggled to concentrate on the task at hand.

Halfway through the book, he stopped, finding what he sought—a remarkable spell, the *Spell of Insight*. It would work better than any other. He read the long list of ingredients and wondered if those were available in the Tower. He shrugged his shoulders. Feeling empowered, he closed the book and placed it carefully back in its secret place.

Yarlen left the room on a mission to retrieve the necessary items. The spell also required the assistance of two other Warlocks. He wondered if the other Warlocks had managed to find the rest of the Guiders to perform the Chant to protect the planet. *'Oh well,'* he thought, no time to worry about that now. It is time to focus on taking care of Alexis and the *Spell of Insight.* It became his priority. He would let Armbruster sleep, for now. *'No need to tell him anything.'* He would wait to speak with him. Armbruster needed rest to regain his energy. He also needed to keep his mind off Alexis and the missing child. *'Best to leave him alone,'* thought Yarlen as he strutted toward the Tower feeling optimistic.

CHAPTER 6

"Tell me where she is! I demand it!"

"You will NEVER see her again," Loggane replied, laughing at the Queen and feeling smug.

"You will surely perish. You realize this, Loggane. I am more powerful than you will ever be. Why even fight me?" Alexis moved her Ceptre over his body and watched as the smoldering sparks made him squirm.

"You didn't think you would get away with this, did you? Silly, little Warlock." Alexis punched Loggane in the stomach with her massive Ceptre. He wailed out in pain but grinned, flashing his teeth at her defiantly.

"You can do whatever you want to me, but you will never find her!" He smirked as he looked up at her, slightly wincing in pain.

"I am losing my patience. What have you done with my daughter?" she screamed, her face inches from his.

"Your daughter is gone forever, Alexis! Trust me, she will have a new life —one without you!" Replied Loggane, a venomous sneer on his face. It was all Alexis could take. She was done—no more games. It was all Alexis could take. She was done—no more games.

Alexis backed up and slammed her Ceptre into his skull. Immediately, Loggane realized those would be the last words he would hear...ever! He faded away slowly, ever so slowly. His world became black. His eyes closed as blood gushed from his head, ending his life.

Alexis stood over him, watching as his life drained away. His hand twitched slightly and then stopped. His foot flopped but quickly ceased to move.

"I told you, you would die! I do not need you. I will find her on my own. I found you, didn't I?" asserted Alexis, feeling powerful, staring at his lifeless body. She shook her head at the insignificant being. Loggane refused to tell her what she needed to know. He was of no use and had to die. It was as simple as that. She did what needed to be done.

Alexis walked out of the room, holding her blood-stained Ceptre high. Even as the blood dripped onto her hand, she snickered with happiness.

It was easy to find Loggane. Her magic worked perfectly. She knew he was not clever enough to stop her. Alexis discovered his whereabouts and expeditiously transported herself to his location. Her spy team informed her that Loggane was responsible for Lilah's kidnapping.

Alexis knew beforehand that she would kill Loggane if he refused to tell her the child's location. She suspected Loggane would refuse to divulge pertinent information. It was not in his nature to be honest.

Alexis was not concerned about the consequences of her actions. She was in charge. No one would question her. She wanted to watch Loggane suffer, withering in pain, as he succumbed to her power. She hoped it would be a slow death. He did not deserve the kindness of an expeditious murder. Loggane should have to endure the same pain she felt at the loss of her missing daughter. She would remind him how it felt and make him realize he had made the worst mistake of his life. Sadly, her team had not yet located the child. Perhaps a spell blocked them from finding her.

Lorthana and Zandorah left the circle feeling empowered. They thanked the others for their help. Once at the top of the stairs, at the entry of the building, Lorthana cast a *Homing Spell*. Instantly, they appeared in Lorthana's home. Once in the sitting room, Zandorah looked at her mom with pride.

"I never knew how much others respect you."

"I was never a useless Witch, Zandi," replied Lorthana, feeling proud and happy. Zandi was her nickname for Zandorah, even though Zandorah was not fond of the name.

"Mom, please stop. I hate it when you call me Zandi. You know that."

"Alright, my love, I will stop. Mothers do that. They call their children by their nicknames. I promise to try and control myself," she giggled, observing her daughter's face.

Zandorah smiled. She didn't hate it as much as she claimed, and she refused to let her mother know.

"Do you think we are safe for now? Should we worry?" Zandorah asked apprehensively.

"I am hopeful the spells have worked. I want to believe we will be okay. Next, we need to find Alexis and Armbruster. I want to speak to Alexis."

"Mom, we cannot appear on Alstromia. You know that."

"Yes, we can. I have a way. Have faith in me!"

"Okay, I will trust you, but I am scared. I am worried about Shawnatar."

"Everything will work out. Shawnatar can take care of himself. He is resourceful."

"Yes, Mom, but he is also still in love with Alexis, which is a problem."

"He loves you, Zandi. Always has, and always will. Believe that."

"You are wrong. Shawnatar loves Alexis. He only married me to make her jealous. I hear him talking in his sleep. He talks about her!"

"Oh, Zandi. I am so sorry. I did not know that."

"It's okay, Mom. I have become used to it. I wanted to believe that over time, he would forget her and let it all go. I hoped he would learn to love me as he loved her."

"... And he will."

"No, he will not. I do not believe that."

"Well, let's not focus on that for the moment."Lorthana reached over and gently touched her daughter's hand. "Let's concentrate on what we need to do. We can worry about Shawnatar and Alexis some other time." She lovingly looked at her daughter. Zandorah nodded but knew things would never be the same. Things had changed, and the future was even more uncertain.

Back at the Palace, Alexis remained alone in her chamber, trying to plot her next step. She ran both hands through her long hair. Alexis closed her eyes with her head tilted up at the ceiling. *'How could Loggane have been so awful? Why did he not tell me where to find my precious girl? What did he think he would accomplish by keeping it from me? He forced me to end his insignificant life. There was no turning back. He sealed his fate with his ignorance and stupidity.'*

She opened her eyes and approached the Eternal Mirror, propped up on the table. Eager to discover information, she stuck her entire head into it. She looked around, hoping for a clue, any sign. The mirror only showed Armbruster conversing with his team. Though she could not hear what they were saying, she knew it was something terrible by their faces.

Irritated, Alexis pulled her head out of the mirror and brushed her hair. *'Why does the mirror always turn my hair ice-cold? It is imperative I find out more about this unique gift.'* It was given to Alexis as a wedding gift by Armbruster's friend and confidant, Yarlen. After brushing her hair, she became hungry and wanted to eat. She summoned Pershiah.

"Bring me something to eat and make it quick. I feel awful. Also, find Aerianna and tell her I want her in my chamber immediately. Do you hear me?" she shrieked at her assistant. Alexis had no patience for someone as slow as Pershiah. The girl moved at only one pace— snail-like.

"Yes, your Royal Highness, your wishes are my command. I will do so immediately," replied Pershiah as she bowed and ran from the room, slamming the massive, heavy door. Immediately, she opened it to apologize, only to have Alexis scream at her to *'GET OUT!'*

Alexis remained in a foul mood. *'Where is Aerianna?'* She expected Aerianna to be more aggressive in her search for answers. Yet, Aerianna had been gone for a long time, failing to report back to her. One thing was for sure, Alexis was sick and tired of all the crap. It seemed like she was the only one taking any action to move things along. Why was it always up to her to make things happen? Why did it seem like she was the only one able to reason and figure things out? *'It shouldn't be so damn complicated,'* she thought. Alexis sat despondently by the window.

Down the hall, in her room, Aerianna finished reading more about the spell. She wanted to ensure she knew all the facts, good and bad, before returning to Alexis. Not knowing all the facts would only irritate Alexis and cause more conflict. Just as she was about to put the book down, suddenly, there was a knock on her chamber door.

"Aerianna, Fanna of Alstromia, you have been summoned by her Majesty, Queen Alexis. She wishes your presence in her chamber at once." Pershiah closed the door and proceeded to the Food Chamber to prepare a meal for Alexis.

Aerianna lifted the *Book of Spells* off the table and decided to meet with Alexis, eager to speak with her. She was a bit nervous about what they would discuss. You never knew what kind of mood Alexis would be in from one moment to the next. It was best to be kind, quiet, and listen most of the time.

"Your Majesty, it is Aerianna. May I enter?" she asked as she knocked on the Queen's door.

"By all means, get in here!" Alexis responded in a huff. "What took you so long? I have been waiting." She looked at Aerianna, annoyed. "You know how much I hate to wait." She impatiently tapped her fingers on her desk, making her point that she was dissatisfied.

"I am so sorry, I came as soon as you summoned me. What can I do for you, Alexis?"

"Do for me? Nothing. It is what we must do. We must do many things. First, I have some tragic news to share with you. I must declare that Loggane is dead. He is gone," she blurted out with a twisted smile, causing Aerianna to frown.

"Uh, what exactly happened to Loggane? How do you know this?" Aerianna responded.

"Are you questioning me?" shouted Alexis, standing up and moving toward Aerianna with her Ceptre extended.

"No, of course not. I would never question you, My Queen. I was just asking if you know what had caused his death."

"My apologies. I am a bit on edge. Please, do not take this personally." Alexis managed a sarcastic smile, sitting down to face Aerieanna.

"So, what do you know, if I may ask?"

"It's all straightforward. Loggane kidnapped my daughter. He refused to tell me where she was hidden, and I ended his life. That's all," she flashed a wicked grin at Aerianna, instantly causing her to feel sick.

'What has Alexis done? Does Armbruster know that she murdered Loggane? This action is permanent. There is no going back!'

"Alexis, Your Majesty – why did you feel the need to do this to Loggane?" inquired a mystified Aerianna.

"Were you not listening? I very clearly told you why," screamed an exasperated Alexis. "What part of *'he kidnapped my child,'* did you not understand? He would not give her back or tell me where she was kept. I had no other choice. I had to do what I had to do." She stood before Aerianna. "Are you going to help me or not? It is your job to be my Second-in-Command and not question me, or do you have a problem with that?" She tilted her head, awaiting a response. Aerianna looked at Alexis in shock. *'What is her problem? I have never seen her act so hostile. Has she lost her ever-loving mind?'*

"Alexis, I have always been by your side. You know I am here for you, no matter what. Of course, I will do as you ask. Whatever you need."

"Okay, then. Let us strategize. How do we want to proceed?"

In the Food Chamber, Pershiah prepared a feast for Alexis. She could have asked one of the other commoners to do so, but she wanted it done right. She placed all the food on a large silver platter, then on a Trillay—a type of cart. She whistled as she walked down the dark corridor, feeling good about the meal she had prepared. Just as she was about to turn to walk down the Royal Hall, she stumbled into Pauto, Princess Lilah's security guard.

"Wow, Pershiah, what's the hurry? You almost ran me over with your Trillay. You need to watch that corner," he joked and smiled, looking at Pershiah.

"I am so very sorry, Pauto. I did not see you. Are you okay?" she asked nervously.

"No harm was done. I am just on edge. I am still looking for clues to help me find the Princess. We are on high alert, and I am exhausted. I could use some food," he gazed at the platter on the Trillay and smiled.

"Oh, no! That is for the Queen. I suggest you back away if you know what is good for you!" She grinned as she slapped his hand away from the Trillay. The two often joked with each other.

Pauto reached over and lightly patted her arm. "I would never. You better hurry and bring her the food, or she will get angry. We all know what happens then," he said, shaking his head and shrugging.

Pershiah knew all too well what he meant. "Have a good night, Pauto." She pushed the Trillay toward the Queen's Chamber. Pauto strolled down the main corridor to find Yarlen and Armbruster.

Alexis fumed. "Where is that worthless girl? I am hungry. It should not take forever to make food. I should have just used magic. She is unbelievable."

Just as Alexis was about to continue her rant, the door opened, and Pershiah entered with the Trillay filled with food.

"Your Majesty, I have brought your food," she announced proudly.

"Well, it is about time. What took you so long? You are the slowest Witch I have ever met. I cannot rely on you, seriously!" Alexis walked toward the Trillay and took in the variety of food with approval. She had to give Pershiah credit. She had made her favorites—Golden Fin Stew with crunchy bread, Vine of Blue in a creamy sauce, and Chocolate imported from Earth. She picked up the skinny, tall glass from the silver tray and took a whiff. It smelled like Porting Wine, a favorite on Alstromia, similar to wine on Earth but much sweeter. She looked happy.

Alexis sat down next to the fireplace to enjoy her meal. Pershiah exited the room, leaving Aerianna and Alexis alone.

"Mmmm, that does smell good. Enjoy your meal. I will leave you to it." Aerianna walked toward the door to leave.

"Excuse me! What are you doing? We are not done here. Just because I am eating does not mean our business is concluded for the night. Please sit down," she motioned for Aerianna to sit next to her on the short, white chair. Aerianna complied reluctantly.

"Okay, I am ready," announced Aerianna.

"Me too...," Alexis smiled as she took a sip of her Porting Wine, then swished it around in her mouth. She was ready to find Loggane's accomplice. There had to be one. She intended to find whoever was part of this conspiracy. It would be fun destroying them the way she killed Loggane. Her malicious grin grew as she nodded at Aerianna, ready to begin plotting their next step.

CHAPTER 7

Marittaz held Essten's hand. She looked sweetly at him. He smiled, but noticed she quickly turned her head away from him. "What is wrong, my wife? Is there something you need to tell me?"

"Essten, I have heard some alarming news," Marittaz said, releasing his hand and folding hers nervously.

"You know, I went to the River of Miccay this afternoon to speak with some commoners about the Pearl Trade, right?" she asked him.

"Yes, of course. You told me you were eager to purchase new pearls for the Torrins. Did something happen?" he asked apprehensively.

"Well, sort of. One of the older women told me how sorry she was for my loss. I was unsure what she meant, so I asked her what she was referring to. The woman looked confused and shook her head. She hugged me and started to cry. I pushed myself away and looked around to see the other women appearing sad, avoiding eye contact with me. The older woman put her hand on my shoulder, stared at me, and whispered, *'They pulled Collan from the river this morning. He is dead.'* I almost fainted. It cannot be true."

"You foolish woman. Those women know nothing! If Collan were dead, we would have been informed."

"I argued with her and said the same thing. The woman assured me she saw his face, though it was bloody and bruised when they pulled him onto the riverbank. It was

Collan. Everyone by the river saw him. The Royal Guards took him back to the Palace."

"LIES! I do not believe it. If so, the King himself would have come to tell me. Armbruster would not keep that secret." Essten tried to convince himself, as well as Marittaz. He had an uncomfortable feeling that she was telling the truth.

"Essten, what if he is really dead?"

"Shut your mouth, woman. I beg you! You are endangering our lives. There is always someone listening." He placed his pointer finger over his mouth, shaking his head. "I will not get tried for treason. I will not accuse our King or Queen of withholding this information! If it is true, there is a logical explanation for why we have not been informed. I'm telling you to shut up and be quiet! We will not discuss this here. I will head to the Palace to speak to Armbruster and find out about Collan. You stay here. Do not, under any circumstances, talk to anyone. Have I made myself clear?" He gave her a stern look.

Marittaz knew he was clearly warning her, realizing it was in her best interest to keep quiet. "I am sorry, Essten. I am just so upset that it might be true. What if our Collan is dead? I am not sure how I can go on. Please forgive me," she began to sob. She put her head on the table and cried loudly.

Essten jumped from the chair and walked to her side. He put his arms around her and gently rocked her as he whispered into her ear, "I promise to find out about Collan. Do not worry."

Essten grasped his patched, frayed, long robe and headed toward the stable. He unbuckled his Torrin and pulled back on the reins, flying high above the Valley of Grandu. Before he knew it, he found himself on the Landing Deck of the Palace. He handed the Torrin over to the Keeper. He smiled and reassured Essten that he would take good care of his Torrin.

Standing before the arch leading to the entrance of the Palace, Essten's hands felt sweaty. His stomach felt uneasy. He was sure of what he was about to hear. Essten desperately attempted to prepare himself from the moment Marittaz informed him about Collan's possible death.

"Your Highness, Essten of the Valley of Grandu is here to see you," announced the commoner.

"See him into my chamber. I do not want to be disturbed," ordered Armbruster.

"Yes, Your Highness."

Essten stared at the oversized, tan chairs by the fireplace. Ornate Ozar candleholders graced the front of the fireplace, glowing with their Purple Flames of Passion.

Obviously, Armbruster had some problems. He would not burn these types of candles unless something were terribly wrong. It was customary to burn the Purple Flames of Passion during times of stress. The scent of the candles had a calming effect.

"Sit down, my friend," requested Armbruster as he pointed to the chair on the left side of the fireplace.

"Thank you. How are you, Sir?"

"I am well. What brings you to the Palace, my friend? Did you locate the mysterious white Torrin?"

"No. I came to ask you a question. I wanted to hear it from you directly," replied Essten.

Armbruster knew instantly what he meant. His heart skipped a beat, caught off guard. He was ill-prepared to tell Essten about Collan.

"What is it, my friend? What may I do for you?" he asked, pretending not to know.

"Tell me. Is it true? Did your guards find my son in the River of Miccay today? Is he truly dead? Please, do not lie to me!" begged Essten, tears welling up in his eyes as his lips quivered.

Armbruster jumped up from his chair and paced around in front of Essten. He stopped in front of Essten and shook his head. Essten instantly realized Armbruster had information about Collan.

"Look, I planned to tell you later today. My guards are trying to clean up his body. We were going to place his body in Visitation Hall, and then inform you about his passing. I did not want you to see him in the condition he was in when he was brought to the Palace. I know you want to see him."

"Sir, did your guards find out what happened?"

"No, we do not yet know. I have every guard trying to get information. I will not rest until we find out something, I promise! You have my word." Armbruster felt horrible.

"Sir, I just want to see my son. Please!"

"Very well. I will have one of my guards take you to Visitation Hall."

"Thank you. You are very kind. I appreciate all you do for my family and me. Please, forgive me," he started to cry. Armbruster pulled Essten close and hugged him. He could only imagine how much this man was hurting—what a tragic loss, his only child!

After a brief moment, Essten stepped back. "I sincerely apologize, Your Majesty. I assure you it won't happen again." He felt a wave of embarrassment, still astonished that he had allowed his feelings to show so openly in front of the king.

"Essten, never apologize for loving your child. I am only sorry I had to tell you about Collan. My heart breaks for you."

Armbruster ordered the guard outside his door to take Essten to Visitation Hall. Meanwhile, he planned to look for Alexis. He wanted to discover what she was doing and why she hadn't attended dinner.

Thunder rumbled outside as Alexis sat in the chamber next to Aerianna, staring out the large window. Alexis glanced at Aerianna, her eyes squinting in such a way, wishing for her to speak. Aerianna had very little to say. Alexis wanted to scream, but kept her thoughts to herself and continued to look outside. She could see the Trimbers sway in the wind as lightning flashed. Alexis grinned, loving the eerie weather. She adored the rain, the howling wind, and the bright flashes of lightning. It reminded her of power, strength, and boldness!

"What do you want to do next, Alexis? We need to talk with Armbruster about Loggane. He has a right to know."

"Have you lost your mind? I am not telling Armbruster about Loggane. Not yet, anyway. The last thing I need is for him to accuse me of acting out of spite. I had every right to take his life. He took my child, and he had to die. Armbruster will not understand. He was close to Loggane. Come to think of it, I will not be telling him. That's the end of it. Stop bringing it up."

Alexis stood up and walked to the fireplace. She placed her hands on her hips, staring intensely into the fire. She tilted her head back and looked up to the ceiling, letting out a long sigh, and spun around. Aerianna looked confounded.

"What is it?"

"I am at a complete loss," declared Alexis.

"And why do you feel that way? I thought we knew what we were going to be doing next?"

"I am talking about Armbruster. I am at a total loss as to what to say to him and what to do about him. I am starting to think he is more than just an inconvenience. He is asking too many questions and causing too many issues."

"What are you saying, Alexis?" asked Aerianna with a look of uncertainty.

"You know exactly what I am saying, Aerianna. He has to be dealt with, one way or another. He can either become a game player, or he will be taken out. He is a liability."

"Wow, I did not realize you hated him so much."

"I never said I hated him. I said he was becoming a liability. If he is not working with me, then he is working against me. Those who work against me will be dealt with accordingly. I do not have the time for indecisiveness. Yarlen is probably already looking into spells to help Armbruster. We must be smarter and quicker than both."

Alexis looked at Aerianna, waiting for a sign of approval. Instead, Aerianna avoided eye contact with Alexis. It only seemed to make Alexis angrier. Frustratedly, she tapped her Ceptre on the table, staring directly at Aerianna.

"Wake up, silly girl. You vowed to protect me, be by my side, and help me in any way you can. Now, you simply look away? Must I now question your loyalty, too?"

"Never! I agree. We will do what we must," concurred Aerianna.

"Good. For a second, I felt rather unhinged. I would hate to think we were not on the same team. Never let me question your loyalty again. Friend or not, I cannot have betrayal in my inner circle."

"You have my loyalty and my life. I promise."

"Tell me about the incantations you have found and what you think we should do next. I also want an update on Zandorah, Lorthana, and Shawnatar. Who is looking into the activities on Earth?"

"I do not have all the answers to these questions, but I promise I will check into it and get back to you as soon as I know something. May I go forth?"

"Oh, I suppose. When you do return, be prepared. I want both spells and the answers about my sister, mother, and Shawnatar. Understood? I am getting tired of repeating myself." Alexis felt displeased. *'Why is this girl turning out to be such a problem? She is supposed to be my Second-in-Command and a leader. She is acting more like a follower.'*

"I will not fail you, My Majesty. I promise." Aerianna stood up and ran from the chamber. She felt her heart beating fast in her chest. She knew she had disappointed Alexis. Aerianna had to make it up to her and regain her trust before facing severe consequences. No one liked the repercussions.

Alexis watched as Aerianna ran from the chamber like a coward. She hated it. More than anything, she disliked what her best friend and confidant had become. *'What is going on? Am I the only one with common sense?'* Alexis desperately wanted to regain control. She shrugged her shoulders and walked to the window. Feeling blasé, she flung herself into her favorite chair.

Alexis picked up her favorite book on the table and read out loud, *"No one is going to hand it to you. Make it happen." 'Hmmm, Earthly wisdom.'* She kept the book from an Earth-dwelling friend. Shell was the most amazing human. She knew precisely who and what Alexis was, but still loved her.

Alexis missed Shell more than she wanted to admit. Shell once told Alexis she would love to accompany her to Alstromia, but knew she would not allow it. Humans and Witches did not mix. It was frowned upon by most Witches and Warlocks. Alexis would not jeopardize her status by allowing a human to enter Alstromia.

Alexis reminisced about a chilly spring day a long time ago when she first met Shell. She had been by the river in New England, walking and searching for wild herbs. She heard a noise as she squatted to pick up a few mushrooms. Startled, she spun around to see a petite, blonde woman staring at her. The woman introduced herself.

"Hi, I am Shell. I did not mean to scare you. I am searching for my dog, Clark. Have you seen him? He is a golden retriever wearing a red collar."

"Ummm, no. I have not seen anyone other than you, that is," Alexis responded.

"Oh, okay. Are you lost? No one ever comes out here. I am surprised to see you."

"I live nearby. I was looking for some wild herbs, berries, and mushrooms."

"I see....so, what is your name?"

"Oh, I am so sorry. How very rude of me. I am Alexis."

"Pleasure to meet you," said Shell, with a gentle smile on her face.

"Well, I best be on my way. I hope you find your dog. It will be dark soon."

"Yes, I know. I hope I find him, too. Maybe we can meet sometime again?"

"You never know. See you later, Shell." Alexis hurried off. Standing beside Shell, she felt an odd but comfortable bond. It confused Alexis. Over time, they became great friends. Leaving Shell on Earth was one of the most challenging decisions of her life. Her heart ached and felt incomplete. Shell was probably one of the only people who knew the real Alexis. Reminiscing about Shell made her smile, but it was also a source of misery at the same time.

'Where is Shell now? Does she still think about me?' Thoughts turned to frustration. Alexis shook her head and tried to erase all thoughts of Shell. *'Why did she come back into my mind?"* Maybe Aerienna's lack of support drove her to think about Shell, the one person

she knew would never betray her. Yet, Alexis had chosen to leave her on Earth.

A loud knock on the door brought Alexis back to reality. She blinked and bellowed, "What is it?"

Ambruster forced open the massive chamber door and entered the chamber. He looked old and drawn. His hair looked frizzy, and his robe was dirty. Noticeably, Armbruster lacked proper personal hygiene and sleep.

"What are you doing?" Alexis interrogated. *'It is way too late for this,'* she thought. She was tired and upset. Alexis wanted to sleep.

"Alexis, we need to talk." He looked at her sternly as he stepped aside. Yarlen jumped out from behind Armbruster. He quickly smacked Alexis in the head with his Ceptre. Before she could say anything, Yarlen chanted the *Spell of Return*. She felt her head become light as air, followed by an intense stabbing pain that made her want to throw up. Within seconds, she fell to the ground and became unconscious. Her limp body was face down on the fluffy rug by the fireplace.

Armbruster dropped to his knees to roll Alexis over. Blood ran down her head and dripped off her face. "What did you do? Are you insane? I did not tell you to kill her!" screamed Armbruster, panicking.

"Relax, Your Majesty. She will be fine." Yarlen reassured the hysterical King.

"What is happening?" shrieked Armbruster as he noticed his wife fading away, becoming a ghostly apparition. He tried to touch her, only to have her fall through his hands like sand…

"She is returning...it is as I planned."

CHAPTER 8

Armbruster looked at Yarlen, horrified. What had he done? Could it be undone? "Yarlen, you must explain." He stared at the ghostly appearance of his wife.

Alexis floated above the ground, hair waving gently from side to side. Her entire being was an icy, blue-gray hue, resembling a beautiful ghost. Her eyes were closed, and her hands dangled limply by her side.

"Sir, I did what had to be done. We had to stop her. You are now back in control. It was what you wanted, no?" Yarlen nervously asked. He thought Armbruster would say something like *'great job, my friend'* or *'finally'*...instead, he seemed upset. What should he say? What could he do? Yarlen was shocked.

"Have you lost your mind? Of course, I am upset. Look at that!" He pointed to Alexis, or what had been Alexis. "You better tell me you can reverse this. I may not be happy with her right now, but this situation is out of control! This is NOT okay. Do you hear me?"

"Armbruster, Your Majesty, I am sorry. I was under the impression you wanted her gone. I thought you wanted her out of the way. This is the only way to accomplish that. She is, or was, so strong. It would have been difficult to control her otherwise. I searched through all the books, and this was the best solution for our situation."

"You are avoiding the point. Is it reversible?" Armbruster flinched, staring at Yarlen, angrier than he had been in a long time.

Apprehensively, Yarlen turned away and began marching around the room in a circle. He refused to look at Armbruster or Alexis. He was unsure of what to say or do. He did not think about it as being a *'reversible spell."* He assumed it was permanent. His first thought was to eliminate Alexis and help Armbruster regain control, thereby restoring him to power. This spell seemed like the most logical way to accomplish that. He spun around and walked toward Armbruster.

"Sir, I do not know. That is my answer. I do not believe we can reverse her condition! I assumed this was in the best interest of our Clan and our new Order. I did what I thought was best. I thought you would be okay with it, especially since she attempted to betray you. You were so upset with her. You wanted to *'kill her,'* so I assumed you wanted me to stop her… no matter how. That is what I did. I did this for you. I am truly sorry that you are mad and upset. I thought you would be pleased."

Armbruster tried to remain calm. He shook his head, wrung his hands, and brushed his hands through his hair. He could not believe what Yarlen had done. Did he hear him correctly? Did he just state Alexis could be like this forever? *'Oh, no, that is not going to happen.'* She was still his wife. Armbruster loved Alexis and wanted her back.

He approached Yarlen. "May I be frank?" he asked with a murderous scowl.

"Of course, Your Majesty."

"If you do not find a way to reverse this incantation, I will do everything in my power to make you suffer the most awful death! DO YOU UNDERSTAND ME?" he screamed.

Yarlen started shaking, almost convulsively. His eyes began to roll to the back of his head, and his mouth began to foam. He dropped to the ground, screaming out in pain, writhing on the ground, unable to breathe.

Armbruster stood over him, chanting, his voice slowly increasing, as did the pain for Yarlen. He allowed the pain to go on for a short while. Then, he walked to the nearest chair and sat down. From there, Armbruster watched as Yarlen picked himself off the floor and stood up, his legs visibly shaking. Yarlen used his Ceptre as a cane to stand. He slowly managed to make it to the door and turned to glare at Armbruster.

"I will find a reversal, I promise. Leave Alexis where she is. I will be back." He limped out the door, slithering down the hall as quickly as possible, considering his legs felt numb.

Armbruster observed Alexis floating above the ground, looking spectral. He couldn't believe what had happened to her. How did he make Yarlen think he wanted this? He never intended to hurt Alexis seriously. Yes, he wished for her to obey and be a loving and caring wife and mother. He stared at her body, swaying lightly, looking peaceful and beautiful. She was a stunningly gorgeous Witch. He continued to observe her from the seat but felt compelled to walk to her side. Once standing over her, he gazed at her with feelings of love.

As he was about to walk back to the chair, he felt a sharp, cold pain in his leg. He looked down to see her ghostly hand in his leg, producing the pain he felt. She seemed *'awake,'* and her eyes were wide open. Alexis had a crazy, wild expression on her face. All of a sudden, he was petrified.

Minutes before, Alexis felt the pain for a second, and then felt her head become light. She imagined it was similar to a floating balloon, unlike her body. She noticed her arms and legs had become paralyzed, dangling like lifeless pieces of flesh. Her eyes would not open. She could hear voices in the background, presumably Yarlen and Armbruster. *'What transpired? Did Yarlen kill me? Am I dead? Why can't I open my eyes?'* She heard Armbruster speaking in an agitated voice.

"Have you lost your mind? Of course, I am upset. Look at that!" Was he talking about her? What did that mean?

"You better tell me you can reverse this. I may not be happy with Alexis right now, but this is out of control! Do you hear me?"

'Hellllooo, I am right here! Why is nobody listening to me? They are talking as if I am not here.' Her head hurt badly. She felt cold and desperately wished that she could crawl into her warm bed and have a nice, warm fire in the fireplace. *'Hmmm, why am I so cold?'*

"Armbruster, Your Majesty, I am sorry. I was under the impression you wanted this. I thought you wanted her out of the way, and this was the only way to do that." Yarlen had said.

'Blah, blah, blah…whatever! Okay, you believed you could get rid of me. I get it,' Alexis thought. She listened to their conversation, still unable to move or open her eyes. She slowly felt her hands move a bit more, her feet wiggling, and her head moving. *'Hmmm, maybe I will wake up and discover this is just a bad dream?'* She could not imagine this being the end. No way, this was not how she would go out permanently! She heard Yarlen leave, and then there was silence in the room.

She quietly whispered, "Come to me, my love," hoping Armbruster would listen to her command. It seemed like an eternity. Then, unexpectedly, Armbruster stood over her. Alexis could feel his presence. She tried to move her arm to reach for his leg.

Suddenly, she felt him move. Alexis opened her eyes, and he noticed. She knew at that instant that Armbruster was not standing over her to protect her. Instead, he was trying to figure out if this was the best way for her to spend the rest of her life. She refused to let that happen. She would find a way to stop all of this and then focus on getting her daughter back.

Aerianna woke up earlier than usual. She spent most of the night before trying to find magical concoctions to beat Yarlen. She did not want to upset Alexis again. There was no way she would let Alexix down. Aerianna would prove herself to the Queen and gain back her trust. She walked to the window and pulled back the heavy, velvet curtains. It still rained, and she immediately missed the sunshine. Alexis preferred gloomy surroundings. The dreary environment highly depressed Aerianna.

The rest of the clan liked weather similar to Earth's. Most of them had become accustomed to Earth's climate and changing seasons. It was nice seeing snow fall from the sky and then experiencing the warmth of the sun. She missed Earth. At first, it had been a refreshing change on Alstromia.

Alexis had allowed the weather conditions to remain as they had been, similar to those on Earth.

Once she implemented the changes, many were displeased about the atmosphere and weather. It was dreary and cold most of the time.

Aerianna walked to her wardrobe and picked out a clean outfit to wear. She dressed in her dark purple robe, feeling most comfortable in it. She slid on matching slippers and picked up her *Book of Spells*. She waved her Ceptre over the bed and ensured it was made and tidy. She aimed the Ceptre at the fireplace to ignite a fire. It was extremely cold in the room. Aerianna left the frigid chamber to head to the library to find out if Alexis was there researching new magic.

Yarlen snored in the black chair tucked in the corner of the library. He had little drops of drool dripping off his chin. Hurting and feeling extremely exhausted, he had fallen asleep. He felt a pulling motion on his arm that startled him. Quickly, his eyes fluttered open. He attempted to focus on the blurry face that appeared before him. Someone handed him his reading glasses, and he placed them on his nose. Looking up, he saw a familiar face.

"Thank you, Aerianna. I appreciate it. I guess I fell asleep." He wiped away the spittle on his face, feeling embarrassed.

"Oh, yes, you were snoring loudly. Goodness, you must have been tired. Why did you not go to your chamber? Are you okay?"

"Yes, I am fine. Why do you ask?"

"It looks like you have black eyes. They are swollen. Are you sure you are okay?"

"I will be fine. No need to worry, child."

"Okay, if you say so. What are you doing here? Anything special?"

"I was researching *Reversal Spells* for a project. I have not been able to find one that will work, though. I need it immediately. It is vital," explained Yarlen, attempting to remain vague.

"What kind of *Reversal Spell?* Can you tell me? Maybe I can be of assistance?" asked a curious Aerianna.

"No, I cannot say…sorry." He had zero intention of sharing anything with her.

"Oh…okay. Well, if you change your mind, let me know."

"I will." He picked up his books and walked out of the library. The last thing he needed was Aerianna asking questions that would only complicate things. He would find Armbruster and tell him about his run-in with Aerianna.

Aerianna sat and leaned back as she watched Yarlen scurry from the library. '*Very suspicious,*' she thought. Something was wrong. He was acting very odd. '*What is happening here? What kind of a Reversal Spell? Why would he need to reverse something? What has he done?*' Aerianna decided to locate Alexis and inform her about this information immediately.

Essten approached the concrete table in the massive Visitation Hall Chamber. There was the lifeless body of his only son, Collan. The lower half of his body was draped in a purple and gold blanket—the Death Sheet, as it was called.

As he approached the table, he felt weak on his knees. He noticed his son's face, almost unrecognizable. Deep lacerations and scratches covered his entire body, indicating he most likely had been dragged along the rocky and treacherous riverbank. His whole face was black and blue. The bruising was extensive. His eyes were forced shut by the excessive swelling. His bottom lip was split open. Essten saw one of his teeth sticking out. It was a dreadful scene. He cried as he looked at his son. *'What a waste of a life. Who has done this to my son, and why?'*

He placed his head on his son's chest and wept. Essten was grateful that Armbruster had requested his body to be cleaned up. He was glad he had not seen it before. This was bad enough.

Deep in the chambers of the dungeon, Aerianna hid two books she found in the library. She did not want Yarlen or anyone else to find them. They had been on the top shelf in the ElderWize section. It was the section containing the oldest and most powerful spells. The black *Book of Spells* was falling apart, but most of the inside was still legible. She wanted to locate something extraordinary, hoping to impress Alexis.

Once the books were safely tucked away in her special hiding spot, she locked the door to the dungeon room. She slid the gold key inside the pocket of her robe, then ran up the long, winding, stone stairway to the main floor. At the top, she glanced around the corner, ensuring no one was there before she came up the stairs. She did not want anyone to see her appear from the dungeons. It would most likely raise suspicion. She did not need that aggravation. Luckily, no one was around.

Aerianna walked up the last step and turned the corner. She headed to the west wing toward Alexis's chamber. A few minutes later, she stood before the door and knocked. She waited, but there was no response. She knocked again and attempted to turn the old, oval knob—nothing. It did not move and appeared to be locked. She pounded the door with her fist.

"Go away! We are sleeping," yelled Armbruster.

Shocked, Aerianna jumped back from the door in disbelief. *'Did he say… We are sleeping? Ummm, since when was he allowed in her chamber? It had been months. Nine or ten months, to be exact.'*

"Sir, I must speak with the Queen."

"I said, GO AWAY. We are sleeping and do not want to be disturbed."

"Yes, Your Majesty. I am so sorry." She walked away, wondering why Armbruster was in the chamber with Alexis, claiming to be sleeping.

Armbruster rolled onto his back. He glanced at Alexis. She floated next to him on the bed, either sleeping or her eyes were just closed. He sighed.

"Alexis, are you sleeping?" he asked her. Yet, there was no response. Concerned, Armbruster looked at her more closely, attempting to see if she was breathing.

"Alexis, answer me, please!" he begged.

"Go away, Armbruster. You did this. Look at me!" Alexis responded angrily.

She spoke! He did not know if he should be happy or worried. "Now, honey…it will be okay, I promise."

"Now, honey? Seriously? This situation is far from okay," snarled Alexis.

Armbruster smirked. He found it somewhat amusing. She seemed harmless in this condition, and for the first time in months, it was a comfortable situation for him. His smile widened. She noticed the smirk and tried to slap his face, but her hand passed right through. Annoyed, she tried again. This time, he felt a sharp pain radiate through his cheek. She grinned the moment she saw him wince.

Their relationship was truly a love-hate one. She started to laugh, and so did he. The two chuckled, then stopped abruptly when there was another knock at the door.

"Your Majesty, we need to speak with you immediately. We have news!"

"I will be right out, Pauto," Armbruster declared. "Alexis, stay here and do not answer the door. I will be back."

"Where would I go like this?" she snidely remarked.

He smiled. "Yes, I suppose you are right. I will be back soon." He jumped off the bed and walked to the door, closing it on the way out. As a precaution, he locked the door from the outside. He did not want anyone to see Alexis in her new condition.

Alone in the room, Alexis stared at the ceiling as she hovered over the bed. She tried to move and sit up, but could not. How could she learn to maneuver in this state? She became beyond frustrated. She did not like being in this condition, unable to move around freely. She closed her eyes and tried to visualize moving toward the chair. She floated over the bed, wanting to scream. *'Why is this not working?'* She shook her head. *'Move already,'* she told herself.

Alexis forced herself to move. Slowly, she managed to get herself into an upright position. She did it! She hovered over the chair and pretended to be seated. She glanced at the fireplace. *'What is Armbruster doing? Where is that worthless girl, Aerianna? Why is she not coming back after Armbruster left?'* She could only assume what Aerianna was thinking about when Armbruster claimed to be sleeping in her chamber. Alexis wanted to laugh.

Down the hall, Aerianna strolled toward her room. She was completely taken aback by Armbruster's presence in the Queen's chamber. *'How is that possible?'* They stopped sleeping together after Lilah was conceived.

Since then, they have lived separate lives. *'Maybe they are back together again? Wait!'* Something occurred to her. *'Why did Alexis not speak when I knocked on the door? Why did Armbruster reply, and there was no sound from Alexis?'* There was something wrong. Alexis would never have allowed it. She would have said something to Aerianna. Alexis would not have permitted Armbruster to speak on her behalf.

Aerianna turned around and ran back to the Queen's chamber. Once she approached the door, she gently knocked three times. She waited for Armbruster to yell. There was no response. She knocked more loudly this time and announced her presence.

"Your Majesty, it is Aerianna. May I enter?"

"Enter, you silly girl," barked Alexis.

Aerianna turned the handle, only to find out it remained locked. "It is locked. Can you please unlock it?"

"Armbruster locked it on his way out. Why don't you cast a spell to unlock it? Gosh, stop being so useless!" complained Alexis.

"Yes, Alexis!" Aerianna raised her Ceptre and chanted. She could hear the lock clanking. Aerianna turned the handle and opened the door. However, before she could open it all the way, Alexis shouted at her.

"Wait! Before you enter, I have to tell you something. Please, do not be afraid."

"Umm, why would I be afraid, Your Majesty? May I enter?"

"Only if you promise not to scream."

"Fine, but you are scaring me." She gently pushed the door open the rest of the way. She turned around, closed the door behind her, and then turned to face Alexis. She stared straight ahead. What she saw utterly confused her. She shook her head and backed up. *'What is that?'* "I do not understand," said Aerianna in a whisper-quiet tone, eyes large in disbelief.

"Yes, thank Yarlen for this one. I believe he used a *Return Spell* on me, also known as the dreaded *Ghosting Spell.* Stop staring at me, for goodness' sake. I am not dead. I am just... sort of not here. Yes, I am here in mind and spirit. Ha-ha, get it...spirit." She started laughing, thinking her comment was humorous, as she watched Aerianna's reaction. She appeared scared, far from amused.

"Alexis, this is not funny! Can this be reversed? I thought the *Ghosting Spell* or the *Return Spell* was permanent. Tell me it is not. This is awful." Aerianna's eyes brimmed with tears. She looked away—her friend, the Queen, a dreaded ghost-like figure. *'How tragic,'* thought Aerianna.

"Stop it, silly girl. I will be fine. I am confident there are spells to reverse it. The question remains, can the idiot find them in time?"

"What do you mean by *'in time'*?"

"Welllll, most of the time, the *Ghosting Spell* has to be reversed in two Earthly days, or it will become permanent. Yarlen better hurry up. Quite a lot of time has already passed, and the clock is ticking, so to speak."

"Are you serious?" screamed Aerianna, scared and distraught.

"Calm down. Yes, I am very serious."

"Well then, what would keep him from reversing it? Maybe he wants you to stay this way? Maybe Armbruster likes you as his new, ghostly wife. Have you thought of that?"

"Okay, you seriously need to relax a bit. Armbruster does not want the mother of his child, or his wife, to be a spirit. What kind of life would that be? Also, once we find our precious daughter, I need to be able to raise her properly. Armbruster knows that all too well. He is not crazy. Sometimes, he is a bit impulsive, but he never wants to harm me. This I know for sure!"

"If you say so, My Queen," retorted Aerianna as she walked closer to Alexis. "May I touch you?"

"Why?"

"Curiosity."

"Oh my gosh, whatever." Alexis extended her hand toward Aerianna, allowing her to touch it gently. Her hand felt like a shard of ice, sharp and cold. Impulsively, Aerianna pulled her hand back from the pain.

"Wow, that is painfully cold. Does it hurt you?" asked Aerianna, frowning.

"Listen up. Enough. Yes, I feel cold. Yes, it is not fun. I hate it. Let's move on. We now have more pressing matters to attend to. I need you to fly to Tullah Mountain and find Florenzzah. She will help you figure out a way to reverse the magic. I do not want to leave it up to Yarlen. He may be good, but he is old and very slow. I do not have time to wait. Time is not on my side. If you have ever wanted to prove yourself to me, now is the time."

"Yes, Your Majesty. I will see her right away. I shall return as quickly as I can. Is there anything I can do for you in the meantime?"

"Not unless you can give me back my body?" whispered Alexis to herself.

"Did you say something, My Queen?"

"Yes, hurry up. Get moving!"

Aerianna bowed and walked out of the chamber. Once she entered her room, she walked to the rickety, old bookshelf by the door, pulling down a bag. She filled it with a few items she thought would be useful for trade with Florenzzah.

Witches always expected something in exchange. Nothing was free. Confidently, she left the room and headed down the corridor toward the landing pad. Arriving a few minutes later, she asked the Keeper to retrieve her Torrin.

Once on the Torrin, she steered it in the direction of Tullah Mountain. She loved flying and feeling the brisk air in her hair, as well as the view from above, looking down at the village below. Huts of commoners lined the riverbank. The wealthier and more fortunate commoners owned mini compounds, comprised of several cabins, which sat side by side. She lifted her head and admired the twin moons, which glowed brightly at night, trying desperately to peek through the cloud cover.

Unlike Earth, there was no sun, and the color of the moons defined the days. During the day, they were a bright teal color.

She could have used magic to teleport herself to Tullah Mountain. However, flying allowed her the opportunity to think. She had much to contemplate and wanted to clear her head before facing Florenzzah.

CHAPTER 9

"She is such a stunning child, don't you think?" Joran asked his wife.

"Oh yes, she certainly is. I only wish we didn't have her here, hidden among us. I prefer not to get caught watching the baby. If the Queen finds out we are holding her child, she will kill us both," Shell fearfully responded.

"Stop saying things like that. No one knows the baby is on Earth. All is well. It is doubtful anyone would suspect she is with humans."

"Alexis knows everything. She has her spies here on Earth. It is only a matter of time before someone figures it all out."

"Relax. No one will ever suspect. Everyone believes you gave birth to her. They have no clue our child was stillborn. Our secret is safe, as is the Princess," declared Joran.

"This is one debt I wish were paid. I dislike this, not at all. I hate lying to our family and friends. I worry about the end result. How will this situation end? I assume, badly!"

"Stop worrying, Shell. You are doing this to save the child and help your best friend."

"I hope you are right. I really do. It feels like a betrayal, and I know Alexis will not tolerate it. She will seek revenge. The last thing I ever want to do is to hurt her," said Shell, feeling sad.

"You are a good and loyal friend. I know this has not been easy for you. However, look at the child. This is the best thing we can do to help Alexis. We saved them both from a vengeful person. In time, you will see this was the best decision. You will learn to accept it. Let us not worry about it for now.

Our priority must be the safety of the child. We absolutely have to do this!"

"I know you are right. It just feels so wrong," professed Shell.

"Rest assured, you are strong and making the right choice. Stop second-guessing the decision we have made. Remember the purpose behind the plan," pointed out Joran, gazing at his wife.

"I love you, Joran. You are correct. I never imagined hurting or disappointing my good friend, Alexis."

"I love you, too. Now, chin up—smile. Let's put *'our'* baby to bed. Let us relax and enjoy this glorious fall day."

They gently placed Lilah in the crib and closed the door. Holding hands, they walked back to the living room. Joran opened the back door, and together, they stepped onto the rear patio. They made their way to the rickety, wooden deck chairs, finally taking a seat.

The trees on the mountain were gloriously colored with shades of orange, red, and yellow. It was a beautiful, crisp day, though the light breeze brought shivers to Shell. She wrapped her shawl more tightly around herself, looking off into the distance, thinking about Alexis. Shell wondered how Alexis coped without her precious child.

Leaves fell from the tree next to her. Shell watched as they gently landed on the ground. She briefly stared at the foliage, still thinking. A hard grip brought her thoughts back to reality.

"Shell, we must get inside. NOW," Joran screamed urgently.

"What is it, Joran?" asked Shell, her head spinning as she tried to figure out what was happening.

"There, look! Off in the distance, on the right," he pointed to a dark cloud. It seemed to glide over the lake. *'How odd!'*

Joran gripped Shell by the arm and pulled her into the house. He closed and locked the door, quickly running to the windows to shut them and pull down the shades. Next, Joran motioned for Shell to sit on the sofa by the fireplace. He placed his finger over his mouth, implying she should remain quiet. She shook her head, not understanding what was happening. He approached and whispered in her ear. "Go see Lilah. Do not make a sound, no matter what you hear. I think they have found us. Go quietly…and swiftly. I love you!"

Joran shoved her toward the nursery, watching as Shell entered and closed the door. He walked cautiously to the window by the kitchen, peeking through the blinds to see what was developing. He observed the cloud turn purple-gray, and it was closer than before. The sky was darker, too. The wind picked up, and leaves hit the window rapidly. He heard the branches scratching the house's side from the massive oak tree by the living room.

Lilah slept on her side, sucking her thumb. She was unaware of what was occurring outside. Shell watched over her nervously. She snuck to the door and listened for unusual noises, but heard nothing.

Anxious, Shell returned to the crib and rubbed Lilah's back. Shell felt sick to her stomach. She could not think, nor could she barely breathe. Shell tiptoed to the window and attempted to peek out. Lifting one of the slats of the wooden blinds, she saw it was raining. She could not see the dark cloud they had spotted earlier by the lake, unaware it was now directly over the house. Shell turned away from the window and headed to the rocking chair. Sitting down and exhausted, Shell pulled the blanket over her lap and covered up, shivering. The room was freezing, and she was frightened. She wondered what was going on in the living room with Joran. *'Is he okay?'* she contemplated.

In the other room, Joran watched as the cloud moved, though he lost sight of it. He assumed it was over the house. The rain was loudly pounding the metal roof and made a clunking noise. He stared at the other side of the room, catching a glimpse of the enormous wall. The fire in the fireplace was almost burned out. Joran decided to light three candles on the fireplace mantle since the room had become dark and gloomy. He threw a large wooden log onto the dying flames, hoping it would reignite the fire. He crumpled up paper for added measure and added it to the fire.

Within a minute, the fire grew to a considerable height. Joran walked to the nursery and quietly opened the door. He noticed Shell was curled up in the chair, sleeping with a blanket. In the crib, Lilah appeared to be sleeping too. Satisfied they were safe, he closed the door and returned to the living room.

Spying out the large window, he hoped to see what had happened to the mysterious cloud. Just as he was about to open the curtain a bit more, a bright light hit his face, blinding him.

He fell backward and tripped, hitting his head on the table and landing on the rug by the sofa. Panicking, he managed to look up. That is when he saw her. He wanted to speak, but his eyes felt heavy, and he reluctantly surrendered to the pain, closing his eyes before muttering a word.

A Witch entered the room alone. She held her massive Ceptre out in front and used a *Bright Spell* to blind Joran. She did not plan for him to hit his head or cause his fall. Apprehensively, she bent down and checked on him. *'His chest is moving. He is still breathing, good!'* She never meant for any of this to happen. *' Where is the child? Where is Shell?'* She left the room to find them.

The first room she encountered was empty, with nothing in the room to indicate life. She closed the door and moved to the next room. It was another bedroom. It, too, was vacant. She proceeded to the next room, opened the door, and smiled. Shell slept in the chair, snoring.

The Witch glanced at the other side of the room and saw the crib. Quietly, she walked to the bed and approvingly nodded. Princess Lilah was curled up on her side, her thumb in her mouth, sleeping peacefully. The Witch hunched down over the crib and picked up the sleeping Princess, wrapped in a tiny cloak. Once she held the child firmly in her arms, she banged her Ceptre on the floor, and they both disappeared.

"Joran, is that you?" Shell looked around, confused. She heard something in the room. Perplexed, she turned on the light and walked to the crib. *'Where is Lilah?'* She frantically ran to the living room.

Instantly, she saw him! Joran was sprawled out on the rug. Shell approached Joran and shook him, frenzied, praying he was still alive.

"Are you okay? Please, please, don't be dead!" she cried. She listened to his chest and could hear him breathing.

"I hear you. Stop shaking me. My head hurts," grumbled Joran. His head pounded, and his arm hurt from her pulling on it so much.

"Thank goodness you are okay. Where is Lilah? Did you hide her?"

"What are you saying, woman? I do not have her. She was with you—in the room! She was sleeping in her crib." He sat up and rubbed his aching head. He felt a massive lump on the side of his skull. Fortunately, there was no blood.

"I assumed you took her when I was sleeping. I woke up, walked to the crib, and found it empty. She is gone!"

"WHAT! What do you mean, gone?" asked Joran, apprehensively

"As I said...she is not in the crib. The nursery is empty!" Frustrated, Shell shook her head. She could not believe what had happened. *'Who took Lilah?'*

"We are in trouble." Joran rubbed his head, looking around. Fearfully, he stared at Shell. She sat on the edge of the couch, wringing her hands in disbelief, terrified. He managed to sit up, squinting his eyes, his neck hurting. "What are we going to do?" Joran asked.

"Do? Nothing. We need to figure out our next step."

"Yes!" he agreed.

CHAPTER 10

"Mom, let me hold her, please!"

"Okay, here you go. Hold her gently." Lorthana handed the baby to Zandorah.

"She does look like Alexis. She is gorgeous. Can we return her to Alexis now?" pleaded Zandorah. The thought of keeping the child away from her sister distressed her.

"No, not yet. We must discover who originally kidnapped Lilah. I am just glad our Clan found the baby. I knew someone would locate her if we put out the word."

"What should we do next?"

"I think we need to find a place to hide Lilah temporarily. We must get in touch with Shawnatar and let him know we are okay. He will be worried," said Lorthana, looking at her daughter with a concerned smile. She knew Zandorah would want Shawnatar to know they were okay. She also assumed that Zandorah felt guilty.

"Mom, stop! I do not want to discuss him." Zandorah turned to walk out the door.

"Where are you going?"

"I am heading to the kitchen to make something to eat. I need to think about how we can keep Lilah safe. We are in great danger. " Zandorah exited the room with her lips pursed. She felt that keeping the child was a horrible idea that would backfire.

Lorthana held Lilah and smiled. The child was sleeping and looked so beautiful. Lorthana held Lilah close to her chest and rocked her, breathing in her smell. *'The baby smell,'* she thought. *'So sweet and innocent.'* She thought about what Zandorah had said. She was right. They were all in grave danger. How would they explain the presence of the child? What would Alexis do if she found out they had Lilah? How would they reunite the child with her parents without endangering their own lives?

Frustrated, she gently placed the child in the middle of the chair by the fireplace. She walked to the window to look outside, overhearing noises coming from the kitchen. Without a doubt, Zandorah was upset. She was making a lot of noise while preparing the food. Pots, pans, and dishes made pinging noises. The cupboard doors slammed. Zandorah was having a heated conversation by herself, loud enough so Lorthana could understand some of the words.

In the kitchen, Zandorah wondered how Lorthana could remain so calm after what they had done. She prepared a simple meal and placed it on the small, round table by the window. Hungry, she sat down to eat. She poured herself a full glass of Porting Wine and sipped it slowly. She started to feel calm coming over her. Suddenly, she had a brilliant idea.

Lorthana picked up Lilah and took her to the bedroom. She placed the still-sleeping child in the small crib by her bed. She pulled the quilted blanket over the child, exited the room, and headed for the kitchen.

"Well, I guess someone is feeling better?" snickered Lorthana as she watched

Zandorah sipping Porting Wine. "You could have told me the food was ready. I am starving."

"I figured you would come into the kitchen after you put Lilah down. Yes, the wine is helping. I have an idea I want to run by you. I think I know what we need to do next."

"Okay, tell me!"

"Why don't you get a plate full of food and a glass of Porting Wine? Then, we will discuss our next step." Lorthana happily obliged.

In the meantime, back on Alstromia, Alexis floated above the chair in her chamber. Her eyes were closed while she attempted to meditate, wishing to relieve the stress. Alexis was keenly aware of noises in the hall, making concentration difficult. She became increasingly annoyed. *'Why is everyone so darn loud and selfish?'* she wondered. All she wanted was silence! Alexis opened her eyes and stared at the door. Suddenly, Aerianna entered.

"Your Majesty, I bring amazing news!" she shouted as she ran into the chamber, almost tripping.

"Goodness, watch yourself. What are you doing?" snapped Alexis.

"Sorry, I was so excited. I just returned from speaking with Florenzzah. I was able to negotiate for the spell. However, we may have an itty-bitty problem."

"Problem? What kind of problem? The last thing I want to hear about is more problems?" Alexis asked, annoyed.

"Well, she wants more than I could give her—she demands you grant her a permanent position on your royal staff."

Immediately after the words left her lips, she knew there would be trouble. Alexis would not take this news lightly.

"Are you out of your mind? I am NOT giving her anything. She should be grateful we came to her and feel honored that I sent you. Who does she think she is? I refuse to be blackmailed."

"Alexis, please hear me out. Florenzzah felt our demand was higher than her payment. She wants to return to your staff. She knows you banned her because of a previous situation. However, she believes this can make you even."

"Even? Ummm, no! We are not even. Not by any means."

"Understood. However, I cannot get the spell from her until you agree to speak with her. Florenzzah is on her way here now. I beg you to please give her what she asks so we can return you to normal. Additionally,

Armbruster is doing as he pleases in your absence. He is again gaining much respect. I am worried he will take power away from you."

"For goodness' sake. I am barely absent, and Armbruster believes he can regain power. I do not think so," shouted Alexis. She raised herself and floated toward Aerianna. She stopped directly in front of her and pointed her finger in Aerianna's direction.

"Listen! I am sick and tired of all the games. Armbruster is not taking anything from me. As far as Florenzzah, bring her to me at once. We will negotiate, and I will address the matter with her later. You get your act together. Ensure Armbruster is under control until I return to work. Got it?"

"Yes, Alexis. Your orders are clear. I shall do as you command." Aerianna turned and sprinted from the room, slamming the door. Alexis floated back to her chair, contemplating the conversation that had just taken place. So, Florenzzah thought she could blackmail her to gain a royal position? *'Really? Not going to happen.'* She was well aware of Florenzzah's powers, but also knew she was not that powerful. She would show the old hag who was the boss. Alexis refused to surrender anything to a puny Witch like

Florenzzah. She would regret the day she attempted to blackmail her.

On Earth, Shell took in her surroundings. The house was empty. She wondered what to do next. They saved the child, only to lose her. In her heart, Shell knew it was essential they send word to Armbruster and tell him everything, though she feared his wrath. She also knew he would not be thrilled and most likely harm her. He was not her biggest fan.

Armbruster felt a deep resentment toward Shell for taking Alexis away from him from the moment they had met. Shell's bond with Alexis was natural and good. They were soulmates, meant to meet. Armbruster disagreed. He felt it was unnatural for them to have such a bond, considering one was human and one was a Witch. He attempted to disrupt their friendship numerous times.

Shell sat on the couch in the living room and stared ahead, not saying a word. Her husband quietly sat next to her and placed his hand on hers.

"Talk to me," Joran insisted.

"No, there is nothing to say. We have to do the right thing."

"And that would be what?" he asked, with a look of fear.

"You know what it is…" she replied.

"I can guess." He knew what Shell was about to say and hated the idea.

"I am sending word to Armbruster. We have to tell him everything."

"Your loyalty is to Alexis, not Armbruster," he reminded her. "I believe you need to rethink your plan, Shell," he pleaded.

"No. It has to be this way. Trust me."

"Okay, I will not question your rationale. I am sure there are reasons why you feel this way. What can I do?"

"You can stay out of it and leave. I do not want you here when Armbruster arrives. I want you to be safe. I will take responsibility for what has happened. I love you," explained Shell, now crying.

He stood up and shook his head. "No way, I am not leaving! We are in this together, Shell. Stop this." He knew his request was futile. She would not budge. The decision was made.

Joran watched as she motioned for him to leave. He nodded and entered the bedroom to gather his belongings while Shell stood and walked to the fireplace. She sat down, crossed her legs, and closed her eyes. Shell thought about Armbruster and how she would explain the situation. She heard the front door close. Joran had left, offended, leaving her to deal with Armbruster as requested.

Shell stood up, walked to the mirror by the front door, and looked at her face. Tears trickled down her cheeks. Fear made her uneasy. She grabbed her long jacket and walked outside, heading into town to find one of the scouts. They would know how to get in touch with Armbruster. As she walked, the wind picked up, the cold stinging her cheeks. She wiped the wet tears away and started to jog toward town, hoping to get there quickly.

The council met in the Main Hall, awaiting Armbruster's arrival. There were a total of twenty-five Guiders, including Armbruster, just enough to enact the *Chant of Reztec.* Alstromia would be secured, taking care of one problem.

The massive chamber doors opened. Armbruster, armed with numerous books, entered, looking flustered.

"Is everyone present? Are we ready?" he barked harshly while surveying the crowd.

Yarlen immediately stood up, nodding. "Yes, Your Majesty. All present. We are ready to proceed."

"Very well. Everyone, one at a time, please introduce yourself to the others." As ordered, each Guilder stated their name, from where they originated, what their specialty was, and finally, how they planned to help.

Finally, the introductions were complete. Yarlen instructed each Guider of their position and what was needed. The plan commenced. After what seemed like a long time, the Guiders stood in a circle with their Ceptres ready for action. Yarlen began the Chant.

Once initiated, no one could stop it. To do so would lead to catastrophe. The Guiders became one, chanting and slamming their powerful Ceptres down. The room began to shake. Colorful swirls of light enveloped the Guiders. Yarlen giggled like a child, knowing the Chant was working. It was complete.

There was a loud banging and hissing noise, followed by extreme darkness. Instantly, the sky turned a deep purple, altering the atmosphere. The planet was finally secure.

Armbruster smiled. The Chant worked like a charm. He approached each Guider and thanked them for their help, reassuring them their service would not be forgotten. He knew he owed them all greatly. The Guiders departed one at a time. Yarlen, however, remained behind. He observed

Armbruster standing before a large window, admiring the purple sky.

"Sir, we have done it."

"Yes, my friend, we have. I could not have done it without you and your team. I am forever in your debt. I promise to make it up to you one day."

"Sir, there is no need. I am only glad we were able to secure Alstromia against our enemies. What shall we do now?"

"We need to resume our hunt for my daughter. Additionally, I need to speak with Alexis. Please look into any news from Earth. Also, since my patience with you is dwindling, I expect you to find a way to reverse her condition expeditiously. I am tired of waiting. The time for her is running out. I may be grateful for your help with the Guiders, but you absolutely must save the Queen. No excuses will be tolerated!"

"I will do so now!" Yarlen took his leave, returning to the Communication Chamber to seek out information that had been received from Earth regarding the missing Princess. He was annoyed that Armbruster remembered the need for the *Reversal Spell* for Alexis. He would have been okay with her staying in her current state. He smiled to himself, thinking it would be better not to let anyone witness his smirk. It could send the wrong message.

Armbruster yearned for alone time to concentrate on drawing up a new plan. He also chose to wait to see Alexis. He was not in the mood to listen to her whining. She would most likely be aggressive. Alexis had not yet been *'returned'* and would be feeling vengeful. Armbruster did not doubt that Yarlen was dragging his feet about finding a *Reversal Spell*, which was why he enlisted the help of Farla, the Great Witch, to help him. Armbruster figured Yarlen would recite a million excuses for why the powerful magic could not be reversed. Armbruster preferred to handle the situation himself from now on.

Alexis admired the purple glow in the sky as she gazed out the window, knowing what it meant. *'Wow, Armbruster and Yarlen pulled it off,'* she thought. She laughed out loud, surprising herself. Sometimes, she regretted not keeping up with Armbruster and his abilities. She had to reconsider his position. He was quite capable. She violently hated Yarlen since his magical powers had placed her in this precarious condition. She vowed to make him pay for his actions.

She sighed, catching a glimpse of the pink, sparkly blanket. She felt like crying, but she couldn't produce a single tear. Alexis missed her precious daughter more than she thought she ever could. It made her feel sick, not knowing where she was or if she was okay. She gazed at the blanket and recalled the day she gave birth. Lilah was wrapped in that blanket, so tiny and vulnerable.

Suddenly, Alexis felt rage. Her green eyes flashed with anger. At that exact moment, there was a loud knock on the door.

"Your Majesty, may we enter?" Alexis knew it was Aerianna.

"By all means, get in here," she shouted. The door opened, and Aerianna entered first, followed by Florenzzah. Aerianna walked confidently and calmly toward Alexis.

"Your Majesty, I bring you Florenzzah of Tullah Mountain." She stepped back to allow Florenzzah to step forward. Florenzzah stood still, unmoving. Aerianna moved in behind her and shoved her toward the Queen. She whispered into her ear, "Don't be stupid."

"Florenzzah, step forward and come before me!" demanded Alexis.

"Your Majesty." Florenzzah bowed and lowered her head respectfully.

"What have you brought me? You see my current situation. I am not in the mood for your blackmail or your arrogance. I expect the *Reversal Spell* immediately," she hissed.

"Your Majesty. I came with the spell but ask for a few things in return."

Alexis moved closer. "Who do you think you are, making demands on me? Do you want to die?" she screamed, watching Florenzzah take a step back.

"Absolutely not, Your Majesty…"

"Silence! Hand Aerianna the spell. Once I am returned, we will negotiate. Not until then. Do you hear me?"

"Yes, Your Majesty." Florenzzah opened her large, black bag and pulled out an ancient scroll. She quickly handed it to Aerianna. Alexis smiled. Finally, everything was about to change!

It was raining on Earth when Shell entered the home and sat on the couch. She felt alone. *'Where is Joran?'* she wondered, missing him already. She figured Armbruster would arrive shortly, and there was no way to mentally prepare for that kind of confrontation.

Nevertheless, she had a plan. Shell was unsure how Armbruster would handle the news, but felt it needed to be done. She stood in the small kitchen, poured a large glass of wine, and awaited his arrival, seated at the table.

On Alstromia, Armbruster sat behind the massive desk in his chamber, reading various documents, when he heard a commanding knock on the door. He sat up and removed his glasses.

"Enter!" he yelled. Yarlen appeared and closed the door.

"Sir, I bring news. I just heard from Senior-Scout Cinderillah. She stated Shell would like a word with you on Earth. She claims to have news about Princess Lilah."

Senior-Scout Cinderillah was a red-haired and feisty Witch. She volunteered to stay on Earth to be Armbruster's eyes and ears. She reported to Yarlen on a weekly basis with updates on what was happening on Earth. She was smart and blended perfectly with the humans. She had a small team of lookouts relaying information to her. Her loyalty was to the Queen and Armbruster.

Cinderillah initiated the communication with Yarlen the minute she received the visit from Shell, requesting to speak directly with Armbruster about the disappearance of the Princess. She knew it was necessary, though she wondered why Shell would know anything about the kidnapping.

Curious, Cinderillah sent out her scouts to dig deeper into what Shell could possibly know. Sadly, she got nowhere in her quest.

Frustrated, she figured it was best to contact Yarlen to inform him of this important event.

"WHAT?" Armbruster instantly stood up and approached Yarlen.

"What do you know?" he interrogated, eager to receive the news.

"Sir, this is the message we received." He handed Armbruster a piece of paper. Armbruster took the note and slid his glasses back on his nose. He read the letter and looked off to the side, his head slightly cocked, thinking.

The message read, *"I respectfully beg your presence. I need to speak with you, Your Majesty. I have information about Princess Lilah. I must insist you visit Earth immediately. If you fail to show, there could be dire consequences for the Princess. - Shell"*

Armbruster nodded. "Have you read it?" he asked, pushing the note toward the old Wizzard and showing him the writing. He then pulled it back and held onto it tightly, like a precious gem in his hand.

"Yes, I have, Your Majesty."

"And…what do you think?"

"Sir, my first thought was that it might be a trap. But, knowing the bond between Alexis and Shell, I must assume otherwise. We must meet with the human and see what she knows. Would you prefer I go in your place?"

"No, we will travel together. I wish to see her for myself. I need to hear what Shell has to say. She would not have risked so much if it were not important. We must depart at once. Please let our command staff know of our decision and initiate the plan immediately," barked Armbruster, eager to head to Earth.

"Agreed. I will return shortly with a strategy." Yarlen left the chamber to find the team and devise a way to appear on Earth without being noticed. Also, they had to figure out how to temporarily bypass the new security measures enabled by using the *Chant of Reztec*.

Armbruster returned to the table and reluctantly sat down, holding the note in his left hand. He removed his glasses, dropped the letter onto the table, and cupped his face with his hands. His emotions overtook him. He sobbed, missing his precious daughter. The thought of finding out what happened to Lilah felt overwhelming. The uncertainty made him feel nauseous. He closed his eyes, still weeping. *'I must inform Alexis,'* he thought. Then it hit him. *'No, I will not tell her until I know more. In her current state, she will lose her mind. She would want to head to Earth in person, but she cannot. No one must know of her current condition.'*

Armbruster knew what needed to be done and was prepared. He stood and approached his closet to change into a different robe. *'Shell darn well better have some real news, or I will end her life.'* He was fed up with all the nonsense. Once and for all, she would prove her loyalty or suffer the ultimate fate.

Armbruster would return with news about Lilah and only then report back to Alexis. Hopefully, it would not be too late to reverse her ghostly condition.

Aerianna and Alexis looked at the spell instructions. It seemed too simple. *'How could it be? There had to be more. There was no way it was this simple. Was it a real spell, or is Florenzzah giving us a fake Spell?'* wondered Aerianna. Both Witches looked at each other, smiling. Aerianna began laughing, and Alexis knew they were thinking the same thing.

"She would not be that stupid, would she?" asked Alexis, a slightly amused look on her face.

"Maybe she believes that if she gives us a fake spell or if it does not work, she has more power to negotiate?"

"Well, we will see. If it does not work, Florenzzah will perish. I am tired of her games. I refuse to accept that she would be so dumb as to try to trick me. She must be crazy. We will deal with her either way. Can you retrieve the necessary items from the Tower? We are almost out of time," Alexis stated.

"Yes, I can get them and will be back shortly. You will be returned to your former self in no time, Alexis."

Aerianna left the room as quickly as possible, heading toward the Tower to gather the necessary ingredients. She wanted nothing more than to return Alexis to her normal physical state without complications.

Alexis looked like a beautiful ghost as she hovered over the chair. She was upright. Her face was a bit twisted, with an awkward smirk. She believed things were about to get serious. It was the calm before the storm. There was no doubt in her mind – she would be that storm! Alexis was about to regain her power! '*Armbruster better enjoy what little time he has left feeling in control because it is about to stop,*' she thought. Alexis was ready to step up and regain her rightful place as the Queen. No one would stop her this time. Yarlen would also pay for his actions. She already had a plan in place for him.

Yes, Alexis figured out Yarlen refused to help change her back. He was blatantly unwilling to find a *Reversal Spell*. She was not stupid. She knew his plan, which is why she implemented her strategy. Now, her plot was almost complete. '*Yarlen, I am coming for you,*' she said, feeling optimistic and in control.

Yarlen and his team devised a cautious plan to make their presence known on Earth in order to interrogate Shell. Additionally, Yarlen discovered a temporary method to bypass the planet's security shield. Aware that urgency was crucial, he understood that everything needed to unfold rapidly.

Not much later, Yarlen made his way to meet with Armbruster in the Main Hall. They would use magic and transport to Earth. Luckily, their departure from Alstromia went unnoticed, leaving everyone oblivious to their actions. It was a secret rendezvous with Shell to discover what she knew about Lilah. They would find out once and for all if she told the truth. Armbruster prepared himself to find out either way.

Unaware of what was happening with Armbruster, Alexis waited impatiently for Aerianna to return with the necessary ingredients to perform her *Reversal Spell*. She looked outside and thought about how odd it was that she was not hungry. When was the last time she consumed food? She missed the taste of food. She longed for many things.

Just as her mind drifted to Lilah again, Aerianna barged through the door, breathless.

"I got it! Are you ready?" she huffed.

"Look at me! What do you think?" snapped Alexis impatiently. "So, what do we do?"

"Very simple. I have already combined everything. We must cast the spell in order, and voilà, you will return," screeched Aerianna, unable to contain her excitement.

"Alright, time is dwindling," Alexis reminded Aerianna.

Seconds later, the two stood across from one another by the fireplace, all items in order. Each item was required to be poured over Alexis as they chanted.

Immediately, Alexis started to feel warm. It was an odd, tingling sensation, as if she had bathed in a hot pool of water. Alexis smiled as she realized she was returning. Aerianna's face reflected what Alexis felt. She could see a bright smile radiating off her friend's face.

"Alexis, you are back! You have returned!"

Elated, Alexis took her right hand and felt her body. Yes, it felt warm and normal. She looked down at her feet, admiring their fleshy color. She strutted across the room to the full-length mirror by the bed to admire herself. *'I'm back,'* she thought, grinning from ear to ear.

Without thinking, Alexis turned around and embraced Aerianna. She felt her friend pulling away, acting awkward.

"I could not have done this without you. I owe you. If I had left it to Yarlen, I would forever be the ghostly figure. I am incredibly proud of you. I am eternally grateful."

"Alexis, My Queen, it was my pleasure. It's good to see you've returned. Now, let's discover what Armbruster and Yarlen are conspiring against you. Something is off. I have not seen them anywhere."

"What do you mean?" Alexis questioned.

"No one has mentioned them in a long time. I asked around to find out where they were and what they were doing. However, even Pauto stated he had not seen either one in a while. I think this is very strange. They must be somewhere. I can only hope all is going well with the hunt for Lilah."

"Odd indeed. We'd better try to locate them as soon as possible! I will head to Armbruster's chamber to talk with him if he is there. You concentrate on finding Yarlen. He is probably still plotting to do something to keep me under his control. Whatever you do, should you find Yarlen, do not tell him of my return. I want to confront the liar myself. We both know it was never his plan to return me to my normal state. He wanted me to remain a ghostly Witch. Trust me. Yarlen will regret his action, or rather, lack thereof."

"Agreed! Shall we meet back here shortly?" inquired Aerianna.

"Yes, we shall."

CHAPTER 11

Yarlen, Armbruster, and their Security Command Team arrived on Earth, outside the small cottage in New England. Luckily, Yarlen's magic cast allowed them to depart from Alstromia. They approached Cinderillah's bright-red front door and gently knocked. The curly, red-headed Witch appeared quickly.

"Your Majesty, Yarlen, please come in," she beckoned for them to enter. She led them into the living quarters of her modest cottage. She pointed to an old, dark-brown couch across from the fireplace.

"Please, have a seat," Cinderillah said humbly.

Armbruster and Yarlen complied and sat down. Both took inventory of the room. Her home was small and cozy but bland. A tiny, circular rug accentuated the center of the room. There was also a table and a chair. The standing lamp in the corner by the window appeared to be broken and crooked. Two large candelabras stood on both sides of the fireplace, surrounded by little vials and various-shaped bottles.

"Sir, I am so happy you decided to come. I have been waiting to see you."

"Yes, we realized it was important, making it our priority to get here right away," replied Armbruster.

"Okay, we are here. Tell us what you know," Yarlen interjected impatiently. He refused to waste time.

"Well, I recently received a visit from Shell. She showed up at my cottage looking awful. She had been crying. I knew something was wrong, so I asked her to come inside. We sat in the kitchen, and she told me she needed to see you. Furthermore, she declared she had critical information to relay. I sent out my scouts to see if they could find out anything about what she had been implying about the kidnapping of your child. However, there was zero news. I am worried. I hope it is not a trap."

Yarlen stood up and started pacing around the room. "Yes, we had the same thought. However, given the relationship between Shell and Alexis, we do not believe it is a trick. We believe she knows something. That is why we are here." He sat back down.

"Listen, we will head to her home to speak with her. We wanted to see if you had any other information before we proceeded to meet with Shell. I thank you for your continued loyalty and friendship. You are a great friend, Cinderillah. Alstromia is grateful."

Armbruster stood up and walked toward the entryway. Yarlen followed, and Cinderillah was right behind them. As Armbruster opened the door to exit, Cinderillah spoke.

"Sir, I would love to accompany you."

Armbruster spun around. "No, you have done your job. We will take care of this. You stay here and remain alert. We need you. We will be in touch."

Respectfully, Cinderillah bowed and thanked them. She closed the door after their speedy departure, pouting and feeling rejected.

Outside, Armbruster, Yarlen, and the Security Command Team briefly discussed the next step. They wanted to be clear on the instructions given by Yarlen. They slammed down their Ceptres and disappeared.

Cinderillah entered the kitchen to pour herself a large glass of Porting Wine. She was grateful that Armbruster trusted her and thanked her for her support. She felt proud, knowing her position on Earth was helpful to the kingdom and the Queen. She still felt uneasy about the Shell situation and hoped all would be okay without adverse repercussions.

Meanwhile, Armbruster, Yarlen, and the Security Command Team arrived outside Shell's modest home. Yarlen instructed the team to secure the building's perimeter and be vigilant for any suspicious activity.

Confidently, Armbruster approached the front door, knocking, staring ahead. Yarlen stood behind him, patiently waiting for Shell to open the door. Suddenly, the door swung open, and Shell appeared. She looked distraught, and her face appeared flushed. She bowed, thanking them for coming, and invited them inside.

Once inside the home, she guided them into a small sitting area located off the left side of the kitchen. She meekly asked if they wanted anything to drink or eat.

"Shell, we thank you for your hospitality, but that is not why we are here. Please, tell us why you summoned us back to Earth," said an intolerant Yarlen. He frowned at Shell, rolling his eyes, and wondered if she was attempting to waste time.

"Your Majesty, Yarlen…I regret to inform you that I have some tragic news to share. I know what happened to the Princess." She swallowed hard and tried not to look away. It was more difficult than she anticipated. She wanted to tell them everything she knew. However, she was also afraid of their reaction.

She continued. "Lilah was kidnapped by Loggane, who used Lilah as a means to make the Queen give him the power he wanted. I believe he thought it was the only way to regain what he thought was rightfully his. After he kidnapped the Princess, I was able to get the child back, with the help of a few Witches I know." She stopped talking. She could see the anger rise in Armbruster's face.

"I intended to protect Lilah. My main objective has been to return her to you and the Queen. My sole purpose was to bring her home safely. However, before I could do so, someone appeared unexpectedly and overpowered Joran, taking her out of the crib while I slept." There it was. She told them the awful truth. She felt queasy. *'What is about to happen to me?'* Shell fretfully wondered. She started to shake but held off the tears, realizing that crying would only make her feel worse. Additionally, they might interpret her tears as a sign of weakness. She did not want that.

"What are you saying?" Armbruster yelled, infuriated. He looked at Shell with disgust. *'Did she retrieve my daughter from Loggane and then lose her? Who has her now?'* His head was spinning, and he became angrier by the second.

Armbruster jumped up from the couch and lunged at Shell. He placed his hand on her shoulder, shaking her violently. Her head flopped from side to side like a broken doll. She did nothing to stop him.

"What is wrong with you, woman? What have you done?" screamed Armbruster.

Yarlen got up quickly. He gently pulled Armbruster's hands away from Shell. "Sir, please," he begged the King. He did not want Armbruster to kill the human. They still needed answers.

Reluctantly, Armbruster let go of Shell, shaking his head with disdain. He thought he would find out where his precious daughter was held, hoping to be reunited with her and to take her back to Alstromia and Alexis. He never thought Shell would betray him or Alexis. At a loss for words, Armbruster chose to sit back down to regain his composure.

"Shell," began Yarlen, "we need to know everything— all the information. Please do not spare us any details. We must find the Princess."

"I have told you everything I know. I have not hidden any other facts from you. I do not know who took her away. Joran said he thought he saw a woman in a long cape, but is unsure. Someone pushed him. He hit his head and passed out. I found him sprawled out on the floor, and he was confused from the head injury. Honestly, that is all I know. I wish there were more."

"Sir, how do you want to proceed?" asked Yarlen, observing Armbruster.

Armbruster sat in silence, contemplating Shell's story. He sat there, saying nothing, looking glum, licking his lips.

Shell started to speak but decided it was best to keep quiet until Armbruster said something. Nervously, she chewed on her bottom lip and stared ahead in silence. A few minutes passed. It seemed like an eternity to Shell.

"I believe we finished here," is all Armbruster said as he stood up, motioning for Yarlen to walk to the door.

"Shell has told us all she knows. We must return to Alstromia. We do not need to be wasting our time here on Earth."

Shell walked behind Yarlen and Armbruster as they headed toward the front door. Yarlen opened the door, allowing Armbruster to exit first. He spun around on his feet to confront Shell.

"Let me be clear, my dear. You had better keep an eye out for anything about the whereabouts of the Princess. Do you understand?" he barked in her face, his eyes squinted, his finger raised.

"Yes, yes, I understand," she stammered, looking away, feeling like a traitor.

Yarlen touched her shoulder. "I know you meant to do the right thing. Nonetheless, we still have no idea where the Princess is, so we are back to square one. Thank you for the information." Yarlen walked outside to join Armbruster and the team. Shell had made a colossal mess out of the situation. Yarlen felt it was only appropriate that he act sternly toward her. She had to learn a lesson from this situation, and he was happy to teach her!

On Alstromia, Alexis sat in front of the dressing table. She looked at the mirror, brushing her straight, black hair. She was back to normal, grateful that her skin was no longer blue. Her thoughts shifted to the traitor, Yarlen, and Alexis smirked. She would make him pay for his betrayal. He would regret the day he attempted to leave her in that awful condition. She knew there was never a plan to *'return'* her. She would make him pay for his disloyalty before his friend, Armbruster. He would witness her power and control over the situation, sending a clear message that she was the only one in charge.

She finished brushing her hair and stood up. As she walked to the side of the table, she grasped her Ceptre and left the room. She proceeded down the hall to find Yarlen and Armbruster. She could not wait to confront and watch them, stunned as they laid eyes on her. They would die from shock alone.

Aerianna ran into Porti and began her interrogation. She insisted he share Armbruster and Yarlen's current whereabouts.

"I have not seen them for hours. I was looking for His Majesty to speak with him about how he wants the Command Team to proceed. We have only vague instructions on how to search for the missing Princess," replied Porti.

"So, no word? That is quite bizarre. I do not like it. Something is wrong. Keep looking. The instant you locate them, find me. The Queen is waiting to speak with them." She walked away. More than ever before, she knew something did not feel right about the situation. *'What are they up to? What do they know that Alexis and I do not?'* It all felt wrong. Her stomach felt peculiar, causing her to stop in her tracks. She trembled slightly but moved on. She wanted to find the two Wizzards and gather more information for Alexis.

"Mom, we need to talk," started Zandorah, looking at her mother. Lorthana held the sleeping baby, cradling her softly against her chest.

Lorthana looked up and smiled. "What is it, Zandi?"

"Mom, I just received word. Shell and Joran spoke to Armbruster. He knows the child was taken from them. He is hunting down the one who has his child. Mom, he is coming for us."

"We have done nothing wrong, Zandi. Calm down. We saved the child, making us heroes. He will thank us. We have absolutely nothing to fear." She tried to reassure her daughter. However, she felt a twinge of uncertainty about her own words.

In the back of her mind, she worried for their safety.

"Excuse me, Mother. We still have Lilah. We should have returned her to Alexis a long time ago. This does not look good. We must bring the Princess back to Alstromia before we are accused of kidnapping her. I do not like this situation at all!" screeched Zandorah. She looked wild-eyed. She paced in a circle while she talked, chewing on her long, red nails.

"Stop it, Zandi. You really must calm down. You will wake the child," demanded Lorthana, getting irritated at her daughter.

"Mom, I am worried sick. I think we need to figure out how to return Lilah. The longer we hold onto her, the more it will appear as if we were part of the original kidnapping plan. It is a dreadful thing."

"I agree with you, honey. I understand your concern. However, I have already begun the process. I have reached out to convey a message to Armbruster. I think it is best to surrender the child to him and allow the King to be the one to bring Lilah to Alexis. It will be done soon."

"What? What plan? Tell me more," insisted Zandorah, curious.

"Sit, my child, and listen up…"

Alexis marched down the hallway, heading for the Main Hall to confront the Security Command Team. She would grill them until someone told her where to find Armbruster and Yarlen. She was pissed off. *'Why did they disappear without sharing their plans? How dare they keep me out of the loop?'* She frowned, feeling disgusted by their lack of fortitude.

The Queen entered the room and immediately noticed Garlow speaking with Pauto. They saw her approach and bowed. "Your Majesty, how may we be of assistance?" asked Pauto, feeling nervous instantly.

"You can start by telling me where I can find my husband and Yarlen," she replied in a huff.

"Your Majesty, we do not know where they are right now. We were deliberating on the situation. No one has seen them in quite some time. Their chambers are empty, and the Ceptres are gone." Pauto shook his head. He knew she was about to scream.

"That is not information, Pauto. We already know that. I would expect you to know their location at all times," she stated with fury.

"My Queen, I can only apologize. I promise my team is actively searching for them, but they may not be on Alstromia!"

"Excuse me? Why do you assume that? Where would they be?" The second the words left her lips, she knew the answer. *'They went to Earth! Why? What is on Earth? Did they receive news about Lilah?'* She felt her face flush. Her heart beat loud and strong. She could feel it in her throat, making it difficult to swallow. Although rage flowed through her body, Alexis tried her best to remain calm. She placed both hands on her hips, staring at the two Warlocks.

"Get your team together and locate them! I do not care where they are—I want them found now!"

'Such incompetence,' Alexis thought. Why did she always have to be the one to do everything? She folded her hands and closed her eyes. *'Calm, stay calm,'* she kept telling herself.

"Yes, My Queen. It shall be done." Pauto instructed his team to prepare for departure to Earth. They planned to find Cinderillah and interrogate her. She was keenly aware of everything happening on Earth and would be their first stop. Everything else would have to wait until they gathered more information.

Alexis turned her back on Pauto and Garlow and returned to her chamber. She hoped Aerianna would be waiting to share information about possible new developments. During the long walk to her chamber, she wondered why nothing worked in her favor.

Aerianna opened the chamber door, searching for Alexis. She was not back. The chamber was empty. What should she do? Just as she was about to leave, Alexis entered the room, looking agitated. Her face was red, her hair looked messy, and she had a scowl on her face as though she wanted to kill someone.

"There you are," she said to Aerianna. "What did you discover?"

"Nothing! No one knows anything. It is as if they both just disappeared. I don't believe they are here on Alstromia. I believe they are on Earth."

"Yes, I agree. I spoke with Pauto and Garlow. They feel the same. They are on their way now to hunt them down. I would like to know what they are doing on Earth. I am frankly shocked they chose to keep me out of their plans. They should have known I would be less than pleased once I got wind of their deceptiveness. Wait and see, Aerianna. They will be sorry. I cannot tell you how tired I am of all this nonsense. The constant lies and deceit. It is getting old."

"What shall we do now, Alexis?"

"Nothing, we must wait. I need to devise a plan to confront Yarlen, reclaim my rightful power, and locate my daughter. I will stay in my chamber. Keep looking and you'll find something. Please report back later tonight. I do not wish to be disturbed unless you have something valuable to share. Okay?"

"Yes, Your Majesty. Enjoy your rest."

"Rest? What is wrong with you? I am not going to rest. For goodness' sake, you are dismissed," she waved her hands, indicating she was discharging Aerianna. Aerianna got the message and left quickly. Alexis was upset. Under the circumstances, it was best to stay out of her way.

Alexis sat on the edge of her bed, staring at the fireplace. The Trimbers burned, crackling, and produced a green and purple glow. She loved the fire. *'Where is Armbruster? He better be on his way back with some useful information,'* she thought. She subconsciously kicked her feet as she sat mesmerized by the flames dancing in the fireplace.

Nothing made sense. Alexis felt tired and wanted to sleep. Still, she knew there was no way she would be able to, even if she tried. Instead, she decided to sit and wait. Someone would eventually bring her newly acquired data. It was just a matter of time.

On Earth, Armbruster's team decided to head back to Alstromia. Having reached a dead end attempting to find the Princess, there was no reason to remain on Earth. Expeditiously, they left Earth, hoping to uncover more clues on Alstromia.

Quickly, they arrived back in the Main Hall of the Palace. Armbruster stood next to Yarlen with a look of defeat on his face. The team remained quiet, awaiting further instructions. The trip to Earth did not turn out as anyone had hoped. Armbruster had no idea what to do and figured Yarlen must feel the same. He could see it on his face. Everyone appeared exhausted.

Armbruster reluctantly spoke up. "I will meet with the Queen and provide her with an update. She must know what we have done and what we have discovered." He felt the conversation would not go well. However, not telling Alexis right away would only infuriate her more. As soon as she found out he was hiding something from her, it would be much worse.

Yarlen grabbed Armbruster's sleeve. "Sir, I do not think that is a wise choice, considering the Queen's current condition," he added, thinking about Alexis in her permanent, ghostly state. He tried desperately to hide his snarky grin.

"No, I must tell her. I will go." He pushed himself away from the table and stood. Armbruster left the room to find Alexis. Yarlen stayed behind to speak with the other team members, instructing them on what must be done next. He wondered what would happen when Alexis realized she was permanently a ghostly figure.

A wave of fear ripped through him, realizing he was in trouble. Alexis would blame him. She would hold him accountable and, most likely, kill him. If she did not kill him, she would make him suffer. Either way, it would not be pleasant.

Armbruster approached the massive door apprehensively. First, how would Alexis feel, knowing her state would now be permanent forever? They failed to reverse her condition. She would be outraged. Second, how would she react to the information he gathered on Earth? Third, would she be upset once he told her about Shell? He realized it had to be done. He opened the door to confront his wife.

Alexis sat kicking her feet, staring at the fireplace, when Armbruster plowed through the door. The instant he saw Alexis in her reinstated glory, he abruptly stopped. He stared at her in disbelief. *'What has happened to Alexis?'* He rubbed his eyes, confused. She could see his perplexed look. She laughed, nodding her head.

"What? You thought I would leave my fate up to you and that worthless, Second-in-Command, Yarlen?" she cackled. "No way. I knew I would only be returned if I placed Aerianna in charge. That girl, she is better than I thought. Close your mouth, Armbruster. It is not a very attractive sight."

"But, but.... how?" he stammered, still shocked and utterly confused.

"Quite simply. My capable friend and confidant conducted extensive research. She managed to locate someone with a *Reversal Spell.* She brought her to me, we negotiated for the *Reversal Spell,* and there you have it. The rest is history," she proclaimed proudly. She knew Armbruster was shocked and reveled in the moment, loving it. *'Nothing better than catching them off guard,'* she thought.

"Honey, I am so happy. This is fantastic!" proclaimed Armbruster as he approached to hug her.

"Oh, stop the act. We both know that you do not care either way. It was apparent from your stunned expression. You expected me to be still the ghostly figure you left. You, as always, underestimate Aerianna and me. You need to get your affairs in order,

Armbruster. I am perplexed at your blatant disregard for me and my well-being." She stood up and walked toward him.

Looking him right in the face, she slapped him hard across his right cheek. Shocked, all he could do was look at her. "You are not the man I married. Where is your loyalty? I hope you enjoyed your little time in charge. It will end now. Get out of here and bring me Yarlen. I have a few things to discuss with your traitorous friend."

"Alexis…." he started to say, rubbing his throbbing cheek. "I have news. I must speak with you." Regardless of how mad she was, he knew it was essential that he shared information with her.

"Unless you know where I can find my daughter, we have nothing to say to each other. You are dismissed." She pointed to the chamber door.

"No, you have to hear this. Sit down!" Armbruster vehemently insisted.

Intrigued, she took a seat and glared at him with her piercing green eyes. He felt a wave of heat rush through him. Armbruster was scared. *'How to start?'* He decided he would start at the beginning when they arrived on Earth.

After a few minutes of recounting every detail, he leaned back in the chair beside the fireplace, awaiting her reaction. She appeared speechless. He expected her to yell, scream, throw an item at him, or do something. But she did nothing, remaining silent. She stared ahead at the fireplace quietly. This was bad. She was never quiet. Quiet was terrifying. Obviously, something horrible was about to happen. Armbruster rubbed his hands together, anticipating the worst.

CHAPTER 12

Alexis slammed down her Ceptre in anger. Instantly, she appeared before Shell's house on Earth. She pounded on the door, almost hurting her hand. The door opened quickly, and a stunned Shell ogled her face. Her eyes bugged out. Shell's body instantly felt like jelly.

"Alexis..." she said quietly, looking down.

"Well, are you going to invite me in, or what?"

"Of course! Please, come in." Shell gestured for her to enter the house. Once inside, Alexis stood in the entryway, facing Shell.

"So, exactly when did you plan to tell me? Did you truly believe that I would not find out?"

"Alexis, let me explain!" begged Shell.

"STOP IT. Stop with the lies. I've had enough. I trusted you!"

"Alexis, everything I did, was for you. I wanted to protect Lilah. I never meant to hurt you. You must believe me. I would never lie to you."

"Sure, I believe you...not," retorted Alexis.

"Listen, I knew you would be upset. I felt it was best to inform Armbruster first. I figured it would be better if he could smooth things over and explain everything to you." Shell stood, leaning against the wall, trying to keep a small distance between them.

"Oh, did you now?" Alexis cringed. "Yeah, well, I find that difficult to believe."

"It seemed like the best plan at the time. Alexis, I honestly believed that I was doing the right thing. I promise." Alexis watched as Shell stood across from her, looking terrified. Alexis waited for a more detailed explanation to follow her comment.

"I realized you would want to know, but I feared your reaction. I messed up. I am very sorry. Please, forgive me."

Tears poured down her face. The emotions overtook her. Alexis remained firm in her stance, unswayed by her fake sobs. Watching Shell, Alexis had the urge to hug her and tell her it was okay, but at the same time, she felt blindsided. Instead, she allowed Shell to cry, standing across from her with her arms firmly crossed, refusing to show compassion.

Alexis continued to observe Shell without saying a word, sending a clear message. Her best friend had betrayed her, and there had to be consequences for such actions.

Shell finally stopped crying and wiped her face with a handkerchief. She looked up at Alexis with an apologetic smile.

"Please, say something—anything!" Shell insisted, pleading with Alexis.

"Exactly what do you expect me to say? You betrayed me? You hurt me? You're a hypocrite? I don't know what you want," hissed Alexis.

"I deserve that! However, my loyalty has always been to you. You must know that. Search your heart!"

Alexis pondered her words. "Yes, I suppose so. I guess I can admit you did the right thing, but in a very twisted and wrong way." Alexis refused to acknowledge she was wrong. She did not admit her faults, especially to a human, no matter what a good friend she had been.

"Come, sit down. Let us talk. I will tell you everything," said Shell. Eager to hear everything, Alexis followed Shell. She planned to remain firm and not allow Shell to make light of such a dire situation.

The two sat down and began a lengthy conversation. Alexis felt at ease. *'Why is it so easy and natural to be here with Shell? Never any expectations, no demands.'* Shell was still one of the best things in her life, and she knew it. The two talked and talked. They even laughed here and there. The friendship was still there. They both felt it.

Armbruster and Yarlen decided that enough time had passed. They needed to locate the other kidnapper. Armbruster cocked his head to the side and smiled at Yarlen. Instantly, Yarlen knew what the King was about to say.

"Lorthana!" the two said in unison.

"Indeed, my friend. We must head to Iriss and speak with her immediately. She has my child. I feel it."

"Agreed. I shall round up the Security Command Team and prepare them for departure." Yarlen left swiftly, feeling refreshed.

Armbruster entered the chamber, hoping to locate Alexis. However, she was not in her room. Immediately, he felt the urge to find Aerianna and force her to divulge Alexis' whereabouts. Eager to speak with Aerianna, he walked down the corridor to her chamber. Aerieanna answered the door, and Armbruster began his relentless interrogation when he stood before her. "Where is she?" he demanded.

Aerianna shrugged her shoulders, confused. "What are you talking about, Your Majesty?"

"I want to know where I can find my wife. You always know her location. Where is she?" Armbruster grew impatient. *'Why is Aerianna pretending she does not know where to find Alexis?'*

"Sir, the last time I saw her, she was in her chamber. I left her there a while ago. Are you sure she is not there?" Aerianna adamantly insisted.

"No, she is not. Very well, I will search for her on my own. If you see Alexis, tell her

I suspect Lilah is on Iriss. I believe she may be with Lorthana." He stormed out of the room, heading to the Main Hall to retrieve his team and depart Alstromia.

Alexis and Shell said their goodbyes. The Queen hoped to return home without incident. Though she had been able to depart the planet with the help of Aerianna, she was still worried. The *Chant of Reztec* was quite powerful, and most spells did not work against it. Luckily, Aerianna's now-deceased mother, Agnessa Moonspell Diamahnte, had been a resourceful and talented Witch.

Aerianna kept her mother's Spellbooks hidden in secret and only accessed them when needed. She was able to locate a Chant in one of her mother's Spellbooks, which counteracted the one in place to protect the Alstromia. Now, Alexis hoped, Aerianna could open a portal to allow her to re-enter Alstromia. Feeling optimistic, Alexis nodded as she slammed down her Star Ceptre.

Instantaneously, she appeared in her chamber with a triumphant grin. She knew where to find Lilah—Lorthana and Zandorah had her. *'Why, though?'* That was the question of the day. She could not understand why they would have taken her baby. *'Does Zandorah feel threatened by the baby, or is she jealous? Why would she stoop so low as to kidnap my child?'* Alexis felt confident that all answers would be revealed soon enough. *'Wait until they see me,'* she thought. *'They will regret the day they kidnapped Lilah.'*

Aerianna entered the chamber and was not surprised to see Alexis sitting quietly in her comfortable chair. She knew that it was a bad sign. She approached without saying a word. Alexis watched Aerianna advance.

"What is it now?" Alexis said with obvious annoyance.

"Your Majesty, I have news. Armbruster just told me he knows where we can find Lilah."

"That is not news. I already know. My child is on Iriss with my mother and sister."

"How do you know this, My Queen?" Aerianna inquired, stunned. *'How does Alexis always know things before I do?'*

"I am not stupid. I can figure these things out on my own. I do not require others to relay information to me."

"Of course, My Queen."

"So, now…get your stuff together. We are heading to Iriss to collect Lilah and discover why these women thought for one second they could kidnap my child."

Armbruster and his team arrived outside Zandorah's Castle. He was grateful Yalen had bypassed the Chant in place, allowing for an immediate departure to Iriss. Armbruster knocked on the Supreme Rulers' Bedroom door, waiting. He could have barged into the room, but he figured he would respect her space. No one came to the door. Frustrated, he pounded more loudly.

Lorthana appeared, opening the door, "We've been expecting you," she said, bowing before him.

"I would think so," countered Armbruster, pushing her aside, forcing his way past her. His security team and Yarlen followed.

Armbruster stopped to stare at Lorthana. She had a blank look on her face and did not move, leaning against a wall.

"I honestly did not know if you would show up. I was worried it would be Alexis. I had hoped it would be you, as I wanted to take the time to explain everything before her arrival. We know she will come."

"Yes, you are better off clarifying it to me. I will not end your life, but Alexis may!"

"Sir, I never intended to do anything to hurt either of you. In fact, Zandorah and I rescued the child from Shell to ensure her safety. Shell retrieved the child from Loggane. So, you see, we worked together to save Lilah," Lorthana rationalized to Armbruster, hoping he would believe her.

"I see. So, you're the hero in this situation? HA! Doubtful," Armbruster responded sarcastically. He shook his head.

"Not really. I am simply a loyal member of your family, protecting you and my grandchild. That is all."

"And Zandorah? Where is she hiding?" Armbruster asked, eager to see his child.

"She is in the other room with Lilah. I asked her to watch the child while I answered the door."

"I demand you bring my child to me right now. Get her. Also, retrieve Zandorah. I have a few choice words for her," screamed Armbruster. He had had enough of all the drivel and lies.

"Yes, I will do so now. Please wait here," Lorthana hurried off.

Armbruster stood by the entry, waiting for Zandorah, Lorthana, and Lilah to appear. Just as he was about to complain to Yarlen, he heard yelling outside the home. He instructed Yarlen to investigate the situation.

Yarlen did not come back inside. Instead, Alexis appeared with Aerianna. Her smug face told him all he needed to know—she figured it out. *'How is she always just only one step behind? She is too smart!'* Armbruster thought.

"There you are, my lovie," Alexis said sarcastically, holding her head high. She glared at Armbruster. "Where is my child? Where are the two worthless Witches?"

"They will be right here. Lorthana has gone to retrieve Lilah and Zandorah." There was nothing else he could say. She already knew, or she would not have come. He rolled his eyes at her. She instantly noticed.

"What, you did not think I knew? How stupid do you think I am? You completely underestimate those loyal to me, Armbruster. When are you going to learn? I am still in control."

"I never thought you were stupid, Alexis. I wanted to protect you. I intended to deliver our child to you. Everything would revert to normal," he explained.

She put up her hand, signaling for him to stop making excuses. "Blah, blah, blah…stop talking. I hear the words, but they mean little. You did not trust me with the truth. We apparently have bigger problems."

Lorthana advanced, holding Lilah in her arms. Zandorah was right behind, hiding nervously. She was apprehensive about what was about to happen.

Alexis stood next to her mother and ripped the baby from her, almost causing Lorthana to fall over. She squinted her eyes at her mom with pure hatred. "How could you?" Alexis hissed at Lorthana. "How dare both of you?" she shouted, looking directly at her sister, wishing she were dead.

"Alexis..." Lorthana started to speak but quickly stopped, knowing anything she said would be futile. Alexis would draw her own conclusions, anyway. There would be no reasoning with her. It was a waste of breath and energy.

Zandorah remained behind Lorthana, silently. She knew this was a horrible situation. She valued her existence and decided to keep her big mouth shut.

Alexis gently kissed the child on the cheek, then handed the baby to Armbruster. Once Lilah was safely in Armbruster's muscular arms, Alexis approached her sister, Zandorah, and pushed her hard.

"So, Sis, what have you got to say for yourself?" Alexis demanded an answer.

"Absolutely nothing. I have nothing to say. Mom already said everything that needed to be said. I love you, Alexis. I have always been there for you and always will be." Zandorah stared at her feet, avoiding eye contact with her sister.

To everyone's surprise, Alexis walked up to Zandorah, grabbed her, and embraced her. She held her tightly.

Lorthana, Aerianna, and Armbruster looked perplexed. That was not the reaction they expected. Lorthana frowned, wondering what Alexis was doing. Something was not right.

"I know, Zandi. I know," Alexis whispered, embracing her sister. The two started crying, another first for them. The others remained silent, watching the scene in utter shock. The group stayed in the living room and spent a considerable amount of time talking. The baby slept quietly in her mother's arms.

Alexis stood up and announced their departure. Zandorah and Lorthana said their goodbyes, still shocked at the positive outcome. Aerianna observed Alexis, holding Lilah, completely confused. There was no way Alexis would be so forgiving and kind toward Zandorah. It had to be a game or a plan. Alexis had been livid, and she would not just forgive and forget.

Alexis and Aerianna arrived at the Palace and headed to the Landing Deck. The two sat on the large concrete bench, enjoying the scenery. Both remained quiet for a while. Aerianna finally spoke. It was killing her. She needed to know why Alexis pretended all was okay with Zandorah. She knew Alexis and was aware of her hatred for her sister. Forgiveness did not come without consequences with Alexis.

Alexis watched the water dance in the fountain. She smiled, feeling cheerful, and eyed Aerianna, but said nothing. Alexis continued to stare at the water, then closed her eyes. She thought about how everything worked out in her favor after all. Nothing was going to stop her. She always had an ulterior motive.

Aerianna observed Alexis, wondering why she chose to forgive Zandorah. The evening was perfect. The breeze was warmer than usual, and the sky was clear. Aerianna couldn't stand it any longer.

"Alexis, Your Majesty, I must know…why did you embrace Zandorah? I know it is none of my business. However, after everything that has transpired, there is no way you are okay with any of it."

"Aerianna, there is a reason you are my Second-in-Command. You know me all too well," snickered Alexis.

"So, will you tell me why?" Aerianna figured Alexis had a secret plan. Of course, Aerianna was eager to learn more about it.

"Zandorah and I will never be okay. She broke my heart and betrayed me. I can play the game just like everyone else. Yes, I could have been harsh and made a scene in front of my family, but why? I believe this was a much better way of handling the situation.

My mother would have been heartbroken. I do not need more drama in my life."

"I see, Alexis." Aerianna nodded.

"Do you? I will deal with Zandorah at a later time. For now, let's just say we are even. I have more pressing issues to contend with…"

"Now what?" questioned Aerianna as she eyed Alexis. She knew Alexis was not ready to share her plan. It was in her best interest to appear concerned, but not overly bossy or nosy. It would only infuriate Alexis.

"Aerianna, we will discuss this further at another time. Let's focus on Armbruster, Yarlen, and the celebration. My child is back. We have much to do. I wish to remain positive for a change." Alexis attempted to look sincere.

"Yes, you are correct, Alexis. We shall focus on better things and put Zandorah on the back burner until you are ready to deal with the situation."

"Deal with the situation? I am ready to deal with it. However, this is not the right moment. We will make a move when I am ready and not before. Is that understood?" Alexis explained, shaking her head.

"Of course, My Queen. I will be ready to come to your aid when you ask. Shall we proceed with the celebration planning?" Aerianna asked, hoping to avoid a confrontation with Alexis. She knew deflection was key. It was always better to stay in good graces with Alexis.

"Yes, let us focus on the festivity. Lastly, we must discuss Yarlen and his betrayal. I will address his disloyalty, and there will be ramifications."

"Of course, Your Majesty. I understand. Please, tell me how I may be of assistance."

"I never thought you'd ask…"

Lorthana and Zandorah stared at each other in disbelief. *'Why is it so easy? Why is Alexis suddenly so forgiving?'* Alexis was not the merciful type. She held grudges and always…always had an ulterior motive.

"Mom, I do not understand. I cannot believe Alexis would let go of her hatred for me so easily. Do you believe she has forgiven me? Can we really move on?" Zandorah remained skeptical. She realized Alexis was stubborn, and giving in or acting lovingly was not her nature. Something about the way things turned out seemed odd and very unlike Alexis. It bothered Zandorah deeply.

"Child, I believe in miracles. Alexis has not always been coldhearted. There was a time when she was loving and kind. She loves you. Do not overanalyze the situation or her actions."

Lorthana wanted to believe Alexis reacted the way she did to make peace. Lorthana felt relieved that the two sisters had gotten along for a bit. She remained hopeful it would stay that way. Lorthana loathed the animosity between them.

"I hope you are right, Mom. I am utterly shocked and cautiously optimistic."

Gardone entered the kitchen, happy to see his wife and daughter. "What are you two lovely Witches discussing?" he inquired.

"We were deliberating about today's events. It is a long story. I hope you have some time," Lorthana said with a smirk.

"Oh, do tell, Hana," Gardone responded, eager to hear the news. He loved gossip.

"I will, dear, at a later time. Where have you been? I was getting worried."

"I have been busy with meetings with my team. Nothing for you to worry about, dear." He hoped to reassure her, but she did not believe him. She squinted her eyes, hating his condescending tone.

"Okay, Gardone. I understand." Lorthana replied. She wholeheartedly felt he was keeping something from her, especially since his answers were evasive.

However, Lorthana did not want to focus on that. She planned to enjoy the moment. For now, her family was happy. Things turned out better than expected, and she refused to allow Gardone to ruin it for her. She would confront him in the future about his long, unexplained absences.

Once back on Alstromia, Armbruster instructed the Guiders to remove the *Chant of Reztec* and give the all-clear. The child was back, and everyone was safe. There was no need for increased protection on the planet.

Armbruster met with his Security Team in Visitation Hall to discuss Collan's death. The group concluded that Collan was an unfortunate victim of circumstance. He witnessed Loggane and his team enter Alstromia and was murdered to keep silent. It allowed them to kidnap the child and escape with enough time to return to Earth undetected.

Armbruster planned to update Essten and Marittaz. He would also ensure they would never have to worry about food, money, or shelter. Essten's family paid the ultimate price for their loyalty to the Queen and Alstromia.

Alexis left the Landing Deck to hurry back to Lilah. She wanted to spend time with her child and enjoy her safe return. When she finally stood over the baby's crib, Alexis adoringly rubbed the baby's feet. She felt her heart melting. It made her realize Lilah was the only good thing to happen to her in a long time. No wonder Loggane used her as a weapon to attempt blackmail. He lost that battle. Alexis took care of him and won. Feeling victorious, she picked up Lilah and held her tightly against her body. Alexis turned Lilah around so the baby faced the massive bedroom window.

"Look, my precious. It is now your kingdom. One day, you will rule it. I will guide and teach you well. You will never have to worry about anything again. I promise!"

The baby let out a small sigh as if she had understood her mother. Alexis felt proud. She felt confident her baby would become a powerful Queen one day. She continued to hold Lilah for a while, wishing that this feeling would never end. Alexis gently played with Lilah's tiny fingers, admiring the child with pure adoration.

After a while, Alexis handed Lilah to Carmin and instructed her to take care of the child. It had been a long time since Alexis felt gratitude and relief. There was just one final step she had to complete—to deal with Yarlen and his ultimate betrayal.

CHAPTER 13

Alexis and Aerianna formulated a plan. It was simple, quick, and precisely the point they wanted to make. They planned an extravagant *'Welcome Home'* celebration for Lilah and her triumphant, safe return. During the elaborate event, Alexis would enact her final plan. It was her Power Play!

Yarlen would once and for all learn never to cross Alexis Snipperdoom again! The invitations were sent, the RSVPs received, and all was ready. The party was about to commence. The Security Team was in place, the mood was cheerful, and Alexis smiled, eager to show everyone her power.

The room was filled with an enormous crowd, and the food overflowed on the tables. There was laughter, creating a joyous atmosphere. Aerianna grinned as she nodded at Alexis. *'Here we go again,'* Aerianna thought.

Once more, Armbruster sat quietly next to Alexis, clueless about what would happen. Yarlen sat next to the King, observing the crowd, unaware of what would occur. He felt confident that everything was back to normal. Earlier in the day, Armbruster informed Yarlen how much he appreciated his aid in rescuing the Princess. Yarlen felt thankful for Armbruster's gratitude and support. He hoped the Queen felt the same.

Aerianna stood. "Ladies and Gentlemen, please be silent! Our Queen has an announcement to make. I ask you to remain hushed as she speaks." She sat down next to Alexis and nodded with approval. Alexis stood up, her palms firmly placed on the table. Forcefully, she pushed her body forward, staring at the crowd.

"Everyone, thank you so much for coming out to welcome back my beautiful daughter! Armbruster and I are so happy and relieved she is home safe. As you have probably heard by now, Loggane attempted to overtake our kingdom, using my child as his weapon of choice. He failed. I ended his worthless and traitorous life. He left me with no choice." She continued.

"Furthermore, we have another among us who also believed he could betray me and get away with it. I assure you, this will never happen. I am not stupid or blind. I have many loyal Clan members on my staff. I can proudly say this with confidence. I know everything." She motioned for her Security Team to approach. They quickly snuck up behind Yarlen, waiting for further instruction from Alexis. Armbruster watched, utterly confused and caught off-guard, frowning.

"Yarlen, you are a traitor. I know what you were planning," she hissed. "I will not elaborate on the trivial details here. We will discuss it at your trial. Frankly, I am shocked you felt the need to double-cross me. You are hereby charged with treason and exiled to the High Tower until your trial. Security, take him away!" She smirked with an evil grin, widening. Finally, Yarlen would know what it meant to have betrayed her. He would be forced to think about his actions as he sat alone, in the High Tower, with little hope of ever experiencing freedom.

The crowd watched as the Command Security Team leader, Pauto Vexxorth, snagged Yarlen's Ceptre from his hand. Yarlen released it without a fight, realizing it was a moot point.

Pauto grabbed the old Warlock by the scruff of his neck and led him toward the door. Yarlen managed to turn around briefly and stare at Alexis. She turned her head away, blatantly ignoring him. "Get moving, Yarlen…" Pauto instructed as he shoved him roughly through the door and out of the Hall. Alexis made her next announcement once Yarlen and the Security Command Team departed.

"So, now that the unpleasantries of the evening are done, please... everyone, enjoy! Let us celebrate why we are gathered here. Have fun." She clapped, beaming with an unmistakable, self-righteous look on her face. Aerianna stood up and clapped as well, showing her support for Alexis. Before too long, the entire room of Witches and Warlocks clapped. The only one not clapping was Armbruster.

Armbruster remained seated, shaking his head, feeling overwhelmed. He assumed Alexis would act against Yarlen but never thought she would throw him in the High

Tower or charge him with treason. Armbruster understood his loyalty to Yarlen would cease immediately. He could not remain devoted to his friend and wife simultaneously. Alexis would not tolerate it and would view such action as a sign of betrayal. He did not want the drama or the heartache. With a heavy heart, Armbruster decided it was best to leave Yarlen in the High Tower for now, without any form of communication.

The trial would be the deciding factor as to whether he would maintain his friendship with Yarlen. Part of him felt guilty. He did not stand up for Yarlen or attempt to save him. However, Armbruster knew it would have been a moot point. Alexis would have completed her plan, regardless. He was no longer in control. She expeditiously completed her plan and regained her power in one very decisive move.

The evening came to an end. The visitors departed, and the clean-up crew quickly returned the Palace to its former glory. They had their orders—to complete the cleanup by the morning. The Queen disliked too much commotion within the Palace walls.

Off in the High Tower, Yarlen sat on a rickety and uncomfortable cot, gazing at the sky through his underwhelming, round window. He speculated Alexis would not end his life. Instead, she would ensure he lived to suffer a drawn-out and destitute existence. He made a colossal mistake, believing himself to be loyal to Armbruster. Armbruster had not yet come to see him, which was a clear indication he was siding with his wife. Yarlen was on his own. There would be a tribunal—a very one-sided trial, for sure. There was no chance he would not be found guilty. He could be stripped of all his magic and weapons if found guilty. Yarlen would face imprisonment in the High Tower for eternity.

Worse, he could be returned to Earth. There, his life would be useless without magic. He knew, either way, he was doomed. Sadly, he had placed his loyalty with someone he trusted, only to have the trust broken. Yarlen became angry, feeling betrayed by his best friend and confidant, Armbruster. He stood up and stretched, thinking he needed to find an ally, someone innovative, inconspicuous, and completely unexpected. He pondered the array of possibilities. Suddenly, a grin covered his face. He knew who it should be. There was no doubt she would do it. She would want revenge as much as Yarlen, knowing what it felt like to be betrayed. *'So, there is hope,'* he said under his breath, feeling optimistic.

Alexis stood near the chamber's fireplace, watching the flames flicker, feeling smug. Everything worked out exactly as she had planned. Her strategy was flawless, as usual. However, she felt a slight twinge that something was not right. She attempted to shake it off. She paced back and forth, still sensing uneasiness. Why did she feel such uncertainty? *'What could possibly be wrong?'* The evening was fantastic, her plan perfect, as always.

Armbruster entered her chamber and approached Alexis. Before she could say anything, he pulled her close and kissed her softly. He ran his fingers through her thick hair. He loved this crazy Witch. Even though he admired her at times, she was one of the most infuriating beings he had ever known.

Yet, he knew it was part of the appeal. It was what drew him close to her. Armbruster was delighted that things seemed to be returning to normal. Perhaps they could move forward and make their kingdom powerful, as they both planned. Alexis did not resist his kiss. Instead, she reciprocated.

They walked hand-in-hand toward her bed, where he pushed her down. He stood before her, flashing her a smile. She opened her arms, ready to make love to him. Waking up in the morning, she stretched and glanced at Armbruster sleeping in her bed. He snored loudly, curled up on his side, facing in her direction. He looked peaceful, warm, and cozy. The comforter was pulled up to his nose, exposing his eyes and forehead.

Alexis scooted toward the edge of the bed, pulled back the heavy blanket, and dashed across the frigid room. She got dressed swiftly, eager to warm up. As she looked at herself in the mirror, she tapped her finger on her lip, lost in happy memories of the night before.

In a hurry, she headed out to find Aerianna, leaving Armbruster asleep. Seconds later, Alexis stood before Aerianna's chamber. Without knocking, Alexis pushed open the creaking, heavy door. Across the room, she spotted Aerianna sitting on the bed. She looked pale, white as a ghost, fidgeting with the sleeve of her robe. Aerianna looked up, her eyes glazed over, obviously deep in thought. She laid eyes on Alexis, contemplating the bad news she was about to share with her.

"Aerianna, what is wrong? Everything worked out as we planned. We had a remarkable evening. Why is your face like that? What is happening? Please, tell me! You look dreadful." Alexis frowned as she observed Aerianna. A wave of panic hit her. She was not prepared for more bad news.

Aerianna reluctantly jumped off the bed and approached Alexis. She reached for her hand, ready to share the news. She swallowed hard and took a deep breath. Now was the time!

"I do not know how to tell you this, but we have a problem. A very, very, big problem! You are not going to like it, not one bit! Perhaps you should sit down, My Queen," Aerianna insisted, pointing to the chair in the corner of the room. Aerianna quickly released the Queen's hand, noticing her nose flaring as anger built.

Alexis puckered her lips as she stepped back, trying to get a better look at Aerianna. She placed her hands on her hips, frowning. Outraged, Alexis continued to observe Aerianna, wondering why she acted strangely. Something was amiss, and she assumed it was disastrous.

"What are you saying? I do not understand! Speak up, you stupid girl. I am not in the mood for guessing games. Hurry and get to the point before I lose my patience!" the Queen screeched.

Alexis bared her teeth, snarling at Aerianna, realizing horrible news was about to be shared, and she was ill-prepared. She was sick and tired of all the recent drama.

With a heavy heart, Aerianna looked directly at Alexis and took a breath, saying:

"Alexis, you better sit down. This may take a while..."

CHECK IT OUT

Be sure to check out all of the books in the Alexis Snipperdoom series.

Book 1 - Power Plays
Book 2 - Enemies from Within
Book 3 - War Becomes Her
Book 4 – Entangled Vengeance
Book 5 – Coming in 2026!

The Magical World of Alexis Snipperdoom: An Official Guide–2023 Edition

www.ingramcontent.com/pod-product-compliance
Lightning Source LLC
LaVergne TN
LVHW100526110826
845146LV00002B/786

* 9 7 9 8 9 9 2 6 7 3 2 4 1 *